AN IMPRUDENT ATTRACTION

Prudence looked at Père Alain riding on the mule beside her and saw a man. A very strong, very handsome man. There were glints of humor in his gray eyes that appealed to her very much. A hood covered his head but she remembered how his thick brown hair shined earlier, in the sunlight.

Prudence shook her head, as if to clear it. "How does a man like you come to be a priest?" she asked.

Père Alain looked startled. He stammered a trifle over his words. But finally they flowed as smoothly as anything else he said.

"A man, any man, becomes a priest in the same way as any other. He is called to it by the Holy Father."

Prudence nodded, yet found herself still wondering if she could trust him. But for all her brave words, she knew it would not be safe for her to travel alone. For now, she had no choice but to trust this man who was both less and more than just a man. And hope he did not guess how much she was drawn to him. . . .

Coming in February

The Beleagured Earl by Allison Lane

Hope Ashburton was dismayed to learn that her family home had been gambled away to a disreputable earl. But the new owner, the notorious Maxwell Longford, seemed genuinely interested in restoring her ruined estate—and stealing her heart, as well....

0-451-19972-3/$4.99

A Worthy Wife by Barbara Metzger

Aurora's fiance was dashing, well-bred—and already married! Fortunately, the scoundrel's brother-in-law was determined to save Aurora from disgrace—even if he had to marry her himself....

0-451-19961-8/$4.99

The Rebellious Twin by Shirley Kennedy

Clarinda and Clarissa Capelle are identical twins—but when it comes to the social graces, they're complete opposites. Especially when they both fall in love...with the same handsome Lord!

0-451-19899-9/$4.99

To order call: 1-800-788-6262

The Sentimental Soldier

April Kihlstrom

A SIGNET BOOK

SIGNET
Published by New American Library, a division of
Penguin Putnam Inc., 375 Hudson Street,
New York, New York 10014, U.S.A.
Penguin Books Ltd, 27 Wrights Lane,
London W8 5TZ, England
Penguin Books Australia Ltd, Ringwood,
Victoria, Australia
Penguin Books Canada Ltd, 10 Alcorn Avenue,
Toronto, Ontario, Canada M4V 3B2
Penguin Books (N.Z.) Ltd, 182–190 Wairau Road,
Auckland 10, New Zealand

Penguin Books Ltd, Registered Offices:
Harmondsworth, Middlesex, England

First published by Signet, an imprint of New American Library,
a division of Penguin Putnam Inc.

First Printing, January 2000
10 9 8 7 6 5 4 3 2 1

Prologue

The Marquess of Wellington, Knight of the Garter, Duque da Victoria, regarded the young officer standing before him with great care. Colonel Harry Langford was a tall man with burnished brown hair and deep gray eyes. He was noted for both his courage and his intelligence, qualities Wellington valued greatly.

"We won," he said.

Colonel Langford nodded.

"We lost too many men," Wellington added.

Again the younger man nodded.

"You think I should follow into France, don't you?"

That startled young Langford into breaking his pose. "That's for you to say, sir," he replied.

"And you'll trust whatever I say?" Wellington persisted. "Oh, do be seated," he said, waving the colonel to a camp chair. "Tell me your thoughts. Your honest thoughts. And tell me what they are saying in camp."

Langford hesitated, but he was not a man who lacked courage, even about this. It was one of the reasons Wellington liked him so much.

"Very well, sir. It looks as though we should follow the enemy into France," Colonel Langford said carefully. "And that is certainly what most of the men are saying."

Wellington shot him a speculative look. "But not you?" he asked shrewdly.

"I think," Langford said, in the same careful way as before, "that things are often not what they seem."

Now Wellington smiled. It was a rare sight these

days, even with the recent victories. "Very good," he said. "And you're right. I've had reports, disturbing reports, of what's going on in the south of France. But I don't know what is happening among the diplomats gathered on the continent. I only know they mean to negotiate treaties that may profoundly affect the direction of this war."

Wellington paused. His hands clasped behind his back, he said soberly, "I've also not had a report through the signal system you and your brothers created in over two weeks. I want you to go into France, make your way to where our man is supposed to be collecting information, and discover what is wrong. I should also like you to set the system going again, if that is possible."

"Certainly sir. If that is what you wish," Langford said, his voice carefully neutral.

Wellington shot him another shrewd look. "Think it's a waste of your talents, don't you? Well, and so it is. I don't mean for you to take over the fellow's post. I want you to take a man with you. He can pass for a native Frenchman and he will take over the post, if need be."

"Why send me at all?"

"Because once you see him to his place, I want you to scout around. See what you can discover." Wellington paused. "This is important, Langford. What I do next will depend a great deal on the information you bring back. Come and look here. I'll show you on the map the areas I am particularly concerned about."

Chapter 1

Miss Prudence Marland stood on the dock in London looking up at her uncle, Lord Marland. She wore the long flowing robes of a Moroccan prince and to all outward appearances she was a slightly built young man. She carried herself, moreover, with an assurance that would have sat well on a man twice the age she appeared to be.

In a voice that carried only to the apparent prince's ears, her uncle said, "I still wish you would change your mind, Prudence, and come to Prussia with me. I need you there, not going off on this mad enterprise."

She shook her head. Her voice was firm as she replied, "You know how inexperienced Stewart is! He needs, we need, to know what is happening in Spain. You know as well as I, Uncle Hugo, that the rumors are most disturbing. Rest assured that I shall join you the moment I know the truth."

The older man reached out and gripped her shoulder. "Be careful," he said, and there was a fierceness in the tone that underlay the words. "We are not in Tangiers anymore, Prudence, and Moulay Soulaiman's guards are not here to protect you. No, nor those of the consul, James Green, either. There, no one would have believed any woman capable of such a masquerade as this. But here, who knows? I do not like this mad scheme of yours. What if you are unmasked? I cannot bear to think of the consequences."

But Prudence met her uncle's gaze calmly and her voice was steady as she replied, "I shall be most careful. Nor shall I be unmasked. Any oddities about my person will surely be ascribed to the simple fact of my being foreign. And you know that as an apparent prince I shall be granted access to Wellington, which I most likely would not be if I were to travel as myself."

"But the risk!"

"Nonetheless," she said, her chin tilted upward in determination, "this is still the safest way for me to travel and the risk must be taken."

The older man sighed again and let go of the other's shoulder. "Very well. But join me as soon as you can. I shan't have a moment's peace until you do."

And then it was time to go. The older man boarded his ship headed to Prussia by way of the North Sea while Prudence boarded one bound for Spain. There were mutterings at the sight of her, but good money had been paid for her passage. Prudence knew the captain was not likely to change his mind and turn her away, no matter how much muttering there might be. Not when the apparent prince was prepared to pay triple the usual rates.

But eyes followed every step Prudence took, her long robes swirling about her as she walked. She was careful to keep her stride long and confident and pretend not to notice the scrutiny she drew. Still, she was grateful when she finally reached the safety and privacy of her cabin.

Neither Prudence nor her uncle spared a glance for the sky. Nor did they know that each of the captains cast a wary eye upward. Or that both men reminded themselves that there was too much money to be made if they sailed with the next tide to be put off by the hint of a storm. Both men were gamblers. And they trusted both their ships and their crews. When the tide turned both set sail.

Colonel Harry Langford frowned. Ahead of him rode Bertrand Vallois, the perfect picture of an aging French school teacher. Harry's own disguise did not sit nearly so well. How on earth had he agreed to let himself be dressed up as a priest and called Père Alain?

It had been Wellington's suggestion, of course. Now who was it had predicted just such a fate for him? Was it his father's friend, Sir Thomas Levenger? No matter, the situation felt very uncomfortable to Harry. But lives were at stake and it was true that no one had bothered them on their journey north.

A small French village came into sight and the other man slowed to let Harry come along side. They watched as several children ran toward them. In flawless French, Harry's companion greeted the children and told them he was a teacher. He did not ask about the heart of their dilemma. He didn't have to.

"*Monsieur,* have you come to help Monsieur Thierry? He broke his leg and lies in bed all day. We have not had a class in weeks."

The colonel let out a silent sigh of relief, careful not to let it be seen. Phillipe was a good man and Harry was relieved to know he was safe.

His companion leaned down and placed a hand on the child's head. "Yes, *mon petit,* we are here to see Monsieur Thierry. Will you show us where he is?"

In answer, the child nodded then turned and headed off at a run.

Harry laughed. He could not help himself. "*Lentement,*" he called out. "Slowly, *mon petit.* We cannot make our mules go as fast as you do."

The boy stopped and grinned cheekily at them over his shoulder, but he did go on at a slower pace. The other children crowded around, also eager to be of service. They chattered about the village, about the injured teacher, about the men who were away at war. And about the rare messages they sent home to their loved ones. It was to these that Harry listened most closely.

Too soon they were at the house where Monsieur

Phillipe Thierry lodged. One of the boys offered to look after the mules for them and the two men agreed.

They found him tucked into bed, an old woman at his side, feeding him soup. His face was drawn into dark lines of resignation. The sight of Langford and his companion, however, changed all that.

The soup was forgotten as the old woman set it aside and hastily wiped her hands on her skirt. She curtseyed to the two men.

Harry's companion greeted her amiably while Harry went to grasp the hand of the man in the bed. In softly spoken French he said, "How are you, my old friend?"

"My leg."

Phillipe Thierry said the two words as if they explained everything. And they did.

"The children told us it was broken. Is it healing well?" Langford asked.

"Healing well enough if I had not injured it all over again. Now I can do naught but stay in this bed all day. I have not been able to watch in far too long."

Harry patted the other man's shoulder. "I've brought someone to help," he said.

"Not you?"

In spite of his obvious pain, the other man's eyes twinkled with mischief. Harry gave a gallic shrug. "Alas, the Holy Father has other plans for me. I was only to accompany Monsieur Bertrand Vallois here and then I am to be away on the Holy Father's business elsewhere."

A quick nod of understanding. An answer equally carefully worded. "But this Monsieur Vallois, he will stay? He can teach the children for me?"

"That is what we plan," Harry answered gravely.

Phillipe sank back against the pillows. "*Bon*. It will do," he said. "When we are alone, later, I shall tell Monsieur Vallois all about the children. And what he must do."

"*Bien*."

Bertrand looked over then and an unspoken message passed between the three men. He and the apparent Père Alain changed places. Harry drew off the older woman, on the pretext of asking about Monsieur Thierry's condition. By the bedside the other two men murmured, as though perhaps Monsieur Thierry and Monsieur Vallois were discussing the children.

Harry knew better. By the time they were done, Bertrand would know all there was to know about Phillipe's responsibilities. He would be prepared, both to be a schoolmaster and to watch for the messages that would be coming from England.

Ah, they had stopped talking. With the smallest nod of his head, Vallois signified that he had the needed information.

"*Merci, ma mère,*" Bertrand told the older woman as he came away from the bedside. "We will leave Monsieur Thierry in your capable care. We will go and prepare the school for classes tomorrow."

The woman's face lit up with a smile. "Classes? You will teach classes? Tomorrow?"

Monsieur Vallois nodded. Again he gave her the courtesy title of mother as he said, "It is past time, do you not think, *ma mère*?"

"Indeed, long past time," she agreed.

They left the small home with a promise to return later, for she assured them she had room for two more guests, and walked the short distance to the schoolhouse.

"Someone has been in here, taking care of this place," Harry said, noticing the well-swept floor.

Bertrand shrugged. "The women of the village. They will have come. In hopes that Monsieur Thierry would soon be able to teach again. You cannot know what it means to them to know their children will learn when they did not have the chance. It is one of the few good things this revolution has done, to bring teachers to all children."

Harry gave his companion a sharp look but said

nothing. Even a monster such as Napoleon, he supposed, could have his good points.

The storm was a fierce one. Standing in the shelter of an outcropping, Bertrand and Harry watched the waves crashing against the shore. Both men seemed impervious to the rain that had already soaked them to the skin.

"There will be no signals tonight," Harry said over the roar of the storm.

Bertrand's lips quirked into a smile. "No. But the sea may yet yield up some surprises."

Harry frowned. "And what has that to do with us?"

"Perhaps nothing. But according to Phillipe, sometimes the surprises are English."

Harry's reply was caught by the wind. But it didn't matter. Because before Bertrand could ask him to repeat it, they both saw something being tumbled toward shore. Harry was the first to realize it was a human being.

In an instant, both men sprang forward to rescue the unfortunate creature from the sea. They waded into the crashing waves and grabbed for the figure and pulled him toward shore.

They pulled the boy, for boy he seemed, far up onto the gravel. "Poor lad, it's a miracle he reached shore, weighed down with these wet robes. As it is, he's half drowned I think," Bertrand said. "We'd best take him back to the village. Though what the locals will make of that, Arab as he is, I can't think."

The boy groaned and they hastily turned him on his side where he spewed up the water he had swallowed. Then in a voice so weak they had to strain to hear, he said, in English, "Where am I?"

Just as softly, but in French, Bertrand replied, "You are in France."

Was that a curse? Harry could not be sure. But a moment later the lad spoke again and his voice was stronger. It was also laced with a trace of fear as he said in French, "Ah, *bon*, I am home then."

Harry looked down at the lad and his voice was dry as he said, in the same language, "We might believe you, my son, if your French was not so execrable."

"And if you were not dressed in the robes of an Arab," Bertrand added, for good measure.

Now the lad struggled to sit. Alarm was patent in his face as he looked at both of them. So was cunning. Harry sighed.

"No more lies, my son," he said gently, still in French. "You are English. Or Arab. Or both. So much we can see. But do not fear, we shall not betray you."

"Why not?" the lad demanded suspiciously.

"Because we do not," Bertrand said, a tremor of both bemusement and amusement in his voice, "betray women, *ma petite*."

Harry gaped at Bertrand then looked more closely at the lad. The boy had lost his head covering and his cropped curls gave him an effeminate look to be sure, but it was the way the wet robes were plastered to the body that truly betrayed the young woman's secret.

Seeing where the apparent priest's gaze had settled, she looked down at her chest. And cursed. Fluently. In a language Harry ought not to have known, but he did.

"You've spent time along the Barbary Coast," he said, startling her. "But I'll vow you were never raised in a harem. Not if you would undertake such a masquerade as this."

It seemed he had rendered her speechless. Perhaps that was just as well. Bertrand took advantage of her silence to discuss possibilities with Harry.

"We cannot take her back to the village," Bertrand said soberly in rapid French.

"What do we do with her then?" Harry replied.

Bertrand raised his eyebrows. "We? Me, I stay. With Monsieur Thierry. But you, you must take her and leave. Tonight. Take both mules. I will bring you food and dry clothes to take with you. But you must be well away before morning. Before anyone sees her. Even now we must move to a safer hiding place. The villagers, they may come to see if anything has washed up on shore. You say she has been on the Barbary Coast, but I'll swear she's English, for all that, and we dare not let her be found."

Harry nodded. He grasped the young woman's hand and pulled her to her feet. When she staggered, he slid an arm around her waist to support her.

"Come. We must do as he says. Quickly."

She came. Either because she trusted these two strange men or because she was too weak to do otherwise. Either way, Harry was grateful she did not stop to argue.

Chapter 2

They rode side by side silently. Harry kept a worried eye on the young woman beside him. She swayed in her seat as though about to fall off the mule at any moment and yet she managed to hang on.

He also waited for the inevitable questions. But there were none. She was as docile as she had been since Bertrand Vallois had given her the nun's robes to wear. Where the man had found them, Harry didn't want to know.

She had not liked them, that much had been evident. Neither Harry nor Bertrand could understand why she should have minded being dressed as a nun. After all, how different could this habit be from the Arabic robes she had been wearing when they found her?

That was still a mystery, but one he did not have time to probe just yet. It was far more important to put distance between themselves and the village. Later he would try to question her further.

As the hours passed and the young woman continued to say nothing, Harry began to wonder if perhaps the enormity of her circumstances had finally reached her. She had courage and determination, he had to grant her that, for whenever he asked if she wished to rest, she refused and urged that they push on farther. Eventually, however, Harry called a halt.

They stopped by a stream well out of sight of the road. It was a place he had stopped with Bertrand on their way north. As they sat side by side, he tried to ask her some questions. She was remarkably reluctant to answer.

"Who are you? And where are you from?"

She tilted her head to study him and for a moment Harry feared she had not understood his French. "Why," she asked at last, in the same language, "should I tell you?"

Harry laughed. "A fair enough question," he agreed. "Perhaps because my friend and I saved your life? Because you have no choice?"

"There are always choices," she countered. "Besides, you are French."

"I am also," Harry said gravely, for he and Bertrand had both agreed it would be best if she did not know the truth, "a priest. And it is therefore my duty to offer you my protection. Come child, do you not wish to make your confession to me?"

"I am not of the Roman church!" she snapped.

Harry shrugged the very gallic shrug that Bertrand had made him practice. "No. But it may help, nonetheless."

She pressed her lips together. "I have nothing to confess," she said.

"Perhaps we should simply begin with names," Harry suggested. "I am Father Alain."

"I am Miss Prudence Marland," she answered, after only a moment's hesitation.

"Prudence?" Harry echoed. "Prudence?" He started laughing. "You masqueraded as a man, you washed up on French shores, and you are called Prudence? You seem singularly misnamed!"

Miss Marland was not amused. She turned to look at him and anger flashed in her dark brown eyes. "Perhaps I was named Prudence with the hope that it would influence my character."

"Perhaps," he agreed, "but that hope seems to have been severely misplaced."

She lost her temper then. Miss Prudence Marland rose to her feet and strode over to her mule. She mounted without waiting for Harry's help, using a handy rock. He made haste to mount his own mule before she could leave him behind.

As they got back onto the road she said, angrily, "I do not care what you think of my name. I dislike you intensely and shan't confide a thing."

Harry could not resist. He lowered his eyes. He sighed. He said in a fatherly voice, "Do you not know, *ma petite,* that such a display of temper is a sin?"

"And dressing me as a nun is not?"

"There were no other clothes to be obtained," Harry snapped in reply. "We told you that. And besides, it is for your protection. God will understand, I assure you."

A sudden thought occurred to Harry. "Do you not wish to live? Were you perhaps a suicide? Is that how you came to be in the water?"

"No!"

Her horrified cry was enough to assure Harry that she meant what she said. And then, almost unwillingly it seemed, she went on.

"The storm was fierce and I stood too close to the rail. The ship tilted to one side and someone, muttering about foreigners and bad luck and storms, seized the chance to push me over. I grabbed for a handhold and instead pulled the man over with me. We were both swept away from the ship in moments."

She paused then added sharply, "And do not tell me I should not have been on deck, for I very well know it. Now. But then I could not resist looking at the sea when it was in such a state."

Harry frowned. Aloud he muttered, "Yes, yes, but what am I to do with you now?"

"Perhaps," she said with a diffidence he would have thought foreign to her nature, "you could point me in the direction of Spain?"

"Spain?" Harry echoed, taken aback.

She shifted uncomfortably in her saddle under his

gaze. "Yes, well, if I could reach the English there they could see me safely home."

"As well ask that I get you to the moon!" Harry countered.

"I must get to Spain," she said seriously.

Harry shook his head. "No. But a smuggler might do. I must find a smuggler willing to take you across the channel and back home."

"I. Must. Get. To. Spain."

This was absurd! Harry thought. Aloud he asked, in his most sardonic voice, "Why? Have you ambitions to become a camp follower to the soldiers there?"

"What if I have?" she asked, a speculative gleam in her eyes.

The devil rose in Harry's breast and he raked her from head to toe before he replied, "You are too spindly. They would not have you."

She gasped in outraged disbelief. She was also patently at a loss for words.

"Good," Harry said. "A smuggler it will be."

She pulled her mule to a halt. "Spain," she said.

"A smuggler."

"Spain."

They glared at one another and Colonel Harry Langford felt a strong urge to strangle the wench. He could just imagine what Wellington would say if he saddled him with the creature by taking her along to Spain! But then his ears caught the sound of horses coming the other way. Instantly Harry was on full alert.

"Quiet, my child," he said softly, in warning. "Do not speak or they will know you are not French."

She glared at him one last time, but not only was she silent, the young woman bowed her head, as though in prayer, so that her face was partially concealed.

Two men, indeed two French soldiers, came around the bend and rode into sight. They pulled their horses to a halt at the sight of the priest and nun on their slowly moving mules. Both men crossed themselves.

"Father, have you seen anyone on this road?" one of the soldiers asked.

Harry shrugged. "A few farmers."

"No sailors?"

"Sailors!" Harry did not have to feign his surprise. "What would a sailor be doing here?"

The soldier hesitated then he, too, gave a gallic shrug. "A man, he is dead now you comprehend, he washed ashore in the storm. We are looking to see if there are any others."

"But why?"

It was the second soldier who answered. "Because he was English."

Harry nodded, his face impassive. He dared not look at the young woman to see if her face betrayed them. Instead he sought to divert their attention to him.

"We have seen no one," Harry said. "But I wish you good hunting."

And then he blessed them, grateful that he had learned his role so carefully.

Once the two soldiers were out of sight, the young woman turned to him accusingly.

"You lied!"

"We," Harry said, careful to stress the word, "have seen no one. He did not ask about me alone."

"Do all priests have such convenient consciences?" she demanded.

Her words stung. Harry would not have expected that. He had, after all, saved her life. And what he did, he did for king and country. Such masquerades had never bothered him before, but still her words stung. So he did what one must in such a circumstance. He went on the attack.

"Do you regret that I rescued you, *ma fille*? And perhaps saved your life again just now?"

"N-no," she conceded. A pause and then she said

with exasperation in her voice, "But I do not understand you and it bothers me!"

That startled Harry into an involuntary laugh. He didn't want to laugh with her. He wanted her off his hands as quickly as possible. What they had just heard from the soldiers would make that far more difficult.

"They will be watching all the ports and even the small beaches where smugglers might put in to shore," she said, almost as though she could read his mind.

"I know."

The irritation in his voice was so marked that it was several moments before she ventured to ask, in a very small voice, "What will you do with me?"

The trouble was, Harry didn't know. "I ought," he muttered, "to put you in a convent until it is safe to find a smuggler to take you back to England. But with your French as bad as it is, I cannot think that would be wise."

"My French will improve," she said meekly.

"Perhaps, but not fast enough. No," he said with a sigh, "you will just have to come with me."

"Where," she asked with a militant gleam in her eye and suspicion in her voice, "are you going?"

Harry gritted his teeth. "Do you know how outrageous you are?" he demanded.

"Yes."

"Don't you care?"

"No. I want to know where you mean to take me," she said without the least trace of embarrassment.

Harry was momentarily speechless. He could scarcely say that he did not know where he was going. Not without explaining who he was and what his mission might be. And that would never do. Finally he fell back on the one excuse that had worked so well so far.

"I go where the Holy Father sends me. I go where the Holy Spirit wills."

She looked at him warily, as if she thought he was

wanting in wits. She even began to shake her head and back her mule away from him.

"I, er, that's all very well for you and I wish you well, Père Alain, but I must get to Spain."

Harry moved with a rapidity belied by his appearance as a priest. He grabbed the bridle on her mule. "Very well," he said, "I see I shall have to take you to Spain."

"Why?"

"Because my conscience will not allow me to let you travel alone. You would be captured and no doubt ravished if I let you go off on your own. No, I will take you to Spain and pray that it is not a disaster for the both of us!"

And if the way was rather roundabout, there was no need for her to know this in advance. But still the confounded young woman was suspicious. Or was that concern he heard in her voice?

"Will it not be dangerous for you?" she asked.

"A priest goes where he must. Even soldiers do not usually interfere."

"Usually?"

Harry shrugged.

Prudence looked at Père Alain riding on the mule beside her and saw a man. A very strong, very handsome man. There were glints of humor in his gray eyes that appealed to her very much. A hood covered his head but she remembered how his thick brown hair shined earlier, in the sunlight.

And now he meant to take her to Spain. Or so he said.

Prudence shook her head, as if to clear it. "How does a man like you come to be a priest?" she asked.

Père Alain looked startled. He stammered a trifle over his words. But finally they flowed as smoothly as anything else he said.

"A man, any man, becomes a priest in the same way as any other. He is called to it by the Holy Father."

Prudence nodded. But she found herself still wondering if she could trust him. "Will you truly take me to Spain?" she asked.

"I have said so, have I not?" the priest demanded, not troubling to hide the irritation in his voice. "And you have no other choice but to trust me."

He was right of course. For all her brave words, Prudence knew it would not be safe for her to travel alone. No, he was right. For now she had no choice but to trust this man who was both less and more than just a man. And hope that he did not guess how much she was drawn to him.

Chapter 3

It was late when they stopped to eat. Harry was careful to choose a clearing that was shielded from anyone traveling on the road. He waited until his companion seemed at ease and then he pressed her for the answers he needed.

"Who, precisely, are you? And why were you dressed as an Arab when we found you?" Harry asked as he handed his companion a chunk of the bread and cheese he had bought from a farmer's wife.

She leaned back against a tree and took a bite before she answered, as though trying to decide how much to tell him. "I was headed to Spain," she said at last. "And it seemed safer, since I was traveling alone, to masquerade as a man. And with the robes of an Arab I felt safer from discovery."

His eyes raked her from head to toe in a way that was most disconcerting. "Even dressed as you are, covered by these shapeless robes, I can tell you are a woman! Whatever possessed you to believe that you could fool anyone into believing you were a lad?"

She flushed. "I am slightly built and I cropped my hair," she said defensively. "I had done it before—quite successfully. Long ago I learned that people see what they expect to see. As an apparent foreign prince, any oddities in how I moved or spoke would be chalked up to that. Or so I hoped."

He eyed her sardonically and waited, knowing it was a most effective technique of eliciting information. And it did so now. After a moment, she sighed and said, "It is very different masquerading as a man, an Arabic man, in England than it was in Morocco."

"Particularly aboard a ship," Harry said with some significance. "At least one sailor concluded you were bad luck and responsible for the storm."

"And pushed me overboard," she murmured.

Harry looked at her closely but did not press her further. He thought she must be close to overwhelmed by her plight. There were shadows in her eyes and he had no wish to find himself with a hysterical creature on his hands.

So instead, in a soft voice that invited confidences, Harry asked, "Why were you going to Spain?"

She hesitated and he wondered what lies she meant to tell him this time. "You might try the truth," Harry suggested with a wry smile.

Startled she looked at him and snapped. "The truth? Why not? I doubt you will believe me anyway. My uncle is a diplomat working for peace."

Harry sat abruptly upright. "A diplomat? What the devil would he be doing in Spain? The peace talks are being held far away from here."

"Do you know," she said, regarding him with a thoughtful gaze, "you swear a great deal for a priest."

Harry flushed and pretended not to hear. To himself he muttered, "Perhaps your uncle was sent to see the king of Spain? But why would he bring his niece with him? Or rather, how could he allow you to travel out to him alone? It makes no sense to me."

She heard him. "I am of age," she said stiffly. "I may travel where I wish."

Harry snorted. "Without a companion or your maid? Dressed as a boy? I have not been gone so long that I will believe this has become the custom for English ladies. Of any age."

"Not gone so long?"

Now it was she who sat up very straight as she repeated his words.

"So you have been in England," she said looking

at Harry with narrowed eyes. "I wonder when. Were you a spy? Collecting information for Napoleon, perhaps?"

It took every ounce of control Harry possessed not to flinch at the word "spy." But he almost laughed aloud at the rest of her conclusions.

Apparently she saw his reaction for she said slowly, "Not a spy for Napoleon. Which I should have known for if you had been, you would have turned me over to the soldiers already, would you not?"

"Perhaps I am merely luring you to a special place of interrogation," Harry suggested. "Or perhaps I hope to lure you into a false sense of safety so that you will confide everything you know into my hearing."

She considered the notion. She studied his face for several long moments and then she shook her head decisively. "No. It is neither of those things."

Harry was startled and amused and touched by her faith in him. He thought her a credulous, heedless, foolish chit of a girl. But nevertheless he was touched. A thought occurred to him.

"You said you were of age. How old are you?"

"Four and twenty," she answered without hesitation or, he would swear, evasion.

Still he was skeptical. "You don't look nearly so old as that," he said.

She grinned. "I know. It is of the greatest advantage to me."

"How so? Never mind, I am not certain I wish to know," Harry said hastily. "But why are you not married? Or are you? Are you trying to reach your husband in Spain?"

The answer should not have mattered to Harry. But unaccountably he found that it did.

"Yes," she said.

"Liar!" he snapped in reply.

Now it was her turn to gape at him. "How can you say so?" she demanded. "You do not know me. How can you possibly think you know the truth of my circumstances?"

"I don't," he agreed curtly. "But I have come to know when you are lying."

Harry stopped and forced himself to fall back into character. He shook his head and let a grave look settle on his face. His voice held a trace of sadness as he said, "Did you truly think, *ma petite,* that I would not know? That my experience as a priest would have taught me nothing about such things?"

She clasped her hands tightly together in her lap. "I forget, sometimes, that you are a priest," she muttered. Then she lifted her eyes to his. "Why did you become a priest?" she demanded.

"You have asked me that before," he reminded her gently.

She tilted up her chin. "I am asking you again. Why did you become a priest?"

This time it was Harry who looked away. He began to gather up the remains of their very simple meal. "One does," he muttered.

She placed a hand over his. "Why?" she asked one more time.

Harry looked at her. There was an earnestness about her that touched some forgotten chord in him and stopped the sharp setdown he had been about to give her.

A wry smile tilted up the corners of his mouth as he replied, finally, "One does as one must. One does one's duty. And when one is called before the Holy Father . . ."

Harry paused and shrugged. He could feel her gaze still searching his face. What was she looking for? he wondered. Without being arrogant he knew that women found him attractive. Was that it? Did she? And if so, what was he to do about it? He dared not risk so much as kissing her. Not in his present disguise. Their journey was perilous enough without any such complications. He cast about for a way to distract her. And himself.

"Here," he said, pulling a knife out of his boot. "I meant to give this to you before."

But instead of taking it, she went very pale and shook her head, almost frantically. "No. I can't. I won't carry a knife."

He stared at her. With more than a trace of impatience in his voice he said, "This is not friendly territory for you and I want you able to defend yourself."

She shook her head again. "I can't," she said.

"Why the devil not?"

She stared at him. "You are a priest, you ought to understand. In my family we do not believe in fighting. Everyone is a diplomat or otherwise dedicated to achieving peace. I will not, I cannot turn my back on all I have been raised to believe. I have never needed to carry a knife before and I will not begin now."

Harry gaped at her. "But your life may be at stake!" he exclaimed.

She stiffened and would not look at him. Instead she stared at her hands and by the way she held herself he could see this was not some foolish whim but a deeply held belief. With a sigh he reached out and took her hand. She did not pull away, though she looked at him warily.

Despite himself, Harry smiled and turned over her hand. Into it he placed the knife and closed her fingers over the handle.

"I should like to think," he said gently, "that I could protect you, if need be. But what if I cannot? Take the knife. Tuck it under your habit. If you choose never to use it, so be it. But for my peace of mind, I wish you to have it. If we are stopped, I shall say you have taken a vow of silence. That way you cannot betray yourself with your French. But if it is not enough well, then, I wish you to be able to protect yourself."

She stared at him with wide, uncertain eyes. He

sighed again and, with a gentleness that sat oddly on his shoulders, he added, "Please? I will not, I cannot travel a step farther with you unless I know you have this knife."

For a long moment, matters hung in the balance. Then, slowly she nodded and pulled her hand away from his. But she still held the knife. And, as he had suggested, she tucked it somewhere on her person, under the nun's habit. Harry let out the breath he did not even realize he had been holding.

"A vow of silence?" she demanded, seizing upon what he had said before.

He shrugged. "What would you?" he asked. "The moment anyone heard you speak, they would know you were not French. And me, I prefer not to deal with the consequences if they did."

She stared at him, then shook her head. "You are the strangest priest I have ever met," she said. "I am beginning to think you have at least as many secrets as I do."

And because that was far too close to the mark for comfort, Harry turned away and busied himself with gathering things up. He let her eat for a few more minutes, then he rose to his feet and said, "It is time we were on our way."

Prudence let her eyes rest on Père Alain far more often than was wise. He was an enigma to her. A priest who carried a knife. A priest who insisted that she carry one as well. She ought to have had the will-power to refuse. And yet there was a comfort in feel-ing the knife at her side. And because the thought disturbed her, she turned her attention back to Père Alain.

Why was he helping an English woman? And why was he free to travel about this way? Why had he not been assigned to a parish church?

She asked her questions aloud. The answers came

almost too quickly. As though he spoke from something learned by rote, rather than from his heart.

"I must help all of God's creatures. So I help you. As for a parish church, the Holy Father has other work for me. He wishes me to travel about. To use my eyes and tell him where his flock has the most need."

There it was again. The sense Prudence had that Père Alain told the truth, but not quite all of the truth. That he shaded it to his own purposes. He did not act like her notion of a priest. But then she knew very little about the church of Rome. Perhaps he was actually very much the typical priest. But somehow Prudence didn't think so.

She shifted in her saddle. "It feels very strange," she grumbled aloud, "to be wearing the robes of a nun. Wrong somehow."

"What do you mean?" he asked, clearly puzzled.

Prudence tried to explain. "I am not the person people think they see," she said. "For that reason, I must admit I am grateful that you choose, Père Alain, to skirt the villages. That you buy or beg our bread and cheese from the farms we have passed instead. I dislike deceiving people in such a way."

"You dressed as a boy," he countered.

"Yes, but then no one thought I was holy or could pray for them."

He was silent for a long moment. Just as Prudence had concluded that he did not mean to answer, he said, "Strangely enough I do understand what you mean. But as I have said before, with your life at stake, I can see no other choice and I do believe that God will forgive you."

Prudence sighed, though she was careful not to let him see her do so. How was it that he knew with such uncanny skill just the right thing to calm her fears? She understood now why people found priests so comforting. Because Père Alain was comforting.

He was also a very comfortable person to travel with. He showed consideration for her at every turn and unlike the gentlemen in England or the various places her uncle had taken her or even the sailors on the ship, Père Alain had no interest in her physical person. Still one thing bothered her.

"Why have you never tried to talk of God to me?" she asked.

He started and looked back at her, over his shoulder. "What?" he demanded.

"I suppose," she went on, as though he had not spoken, "that perhaps you consider me a hopeless proposition? My soul, I mean. Still, one might think you would at least have tried to save my soul."

He gaped at her a moment longer and then he looked away. Was that chagrin in his expression? Prudence allowed herself a moment of satisfaction. But then his shoulders began to shake with what she was certain was silent laughter.

So he thought her absurd? She would not, Prudence vowed, let him ever know how much that notion hurt. When she was certain her voice would sound steady and perhaps even a trifle heedless, she asked, "Where will we stop for the night? And how soon?"

He looked up at the sky before he answered. "Somewhere with shelter. It will rain again, I fear."

"So a barn," she said.

He shrugged. "Yes, perhaps a barn. But only if we are very, very lucky."

Chapter 4

Philip and James Langford, brothers to Colonel Harry Langford, looked at one another, then at Sir Thomas Levenger. "Are you absolutely certain, sir?" Philip asked.

Sir Thomas turned his hand one way, then the other. "How can one be entirely certain of anything? But the word I have is that this letter disappeared almost ten years ago." He paused and looked at James. "And you are certain it was found hidden among your father's possessions? Forgive me for suggesting such a thing, but are you certain your wife did not bring it with her?"

James smiled. "Both her maid and my valet saw the mirror come apart. My father's mirror. It was most cunningly designed to do so, you know. And hidden inside was the letter. Both of them saw her find it and would swear it came as a complete surprise to her. But what does it mean? Surely by now you must have some notion?"

Sir Thomas nodded gravely. "Yes, but I am not allowed to tell you anything about it."

"What?" Philip thundered his outrage. "But that is unconscionable! This touches on our father's honor!"

"It is necessary," Sir Thomas countered in his calm, quiet voice. "I can only tell you that there was more to the letter than a mere greeting between friends, even if one of them was Napoleon Bonaparte."

"A code?" Philip asked.

Sir Thomas, one of England's most distinguished

and respected judges, merely smiled and ignored the question. Instead he asked in what both Langford brothers knew to be a deceptively careless voice, "Have either of you had word from your brother Harry of late?"

"Not for some time. We've no notion where he is or what he is doing or even if he is safe," James replied, frustration patent in his voice.

"And the signals? They are still going out as arranged?" Sir Thomas persisted.

Philip and James looked at one another, thoroughly confused by now.

"Emily is writing the messages she is given into her stories for the paper, just as she has been doing since we began this mad enterprise, at Harry's request," Philip answered slowly.

"And I checked on the tower only last week," James added. "I took Baines some new lenses to use to make the signals from Dover Castle. He said the man there is doing his job precisely as instructed."

Sir Thomas nodded. "Well, no doubt there is nothing to worry about. No doubt one of us will soon hear that everything is all right and none of us need worry."

The note of false heartiness and reassurance in the barrister's voice alarmed the two Langford brothers almost more than anything else could have.

"Now remember! You have taken a vow of silence. Do not speak a word," Harry warned.

She didn't like the notion, he could see it in her face, but there was no time to argue. A small group of soldiers led by an officer came into sight. An officer who knew Harry. They recognized each other at precisely the same moment. And the officer was faster for he did not have to fumble beneath a priest's robe to retrieve his pistols.

"Well, well, what is an English officer doing so far from England? Or even Spain?" the French officer asked, his own pistol pointed straight at Harry's heart.

Harry did not answer. Not even when he heard the squeak of angry surprise from the woman beside him. The French officer turned his attention to her.

"And who is this?" he asked.

It wasn't going to work. Harry knew that, but still he tried. "She is a nun who has taken a vow of silence," he said, with a pretend indifference in his voice.

"As you are a priest?" the Frenchman countered.

"I stopped at a convent. They asked me to escort her to another. I agreed because I thought it would help my disguise," Harry said with a careless shrug.

The officer looked at the young woman carefully, then back at Harry. "Which convent?" he demanded. "And to what convent were you to deliver her?"

For a moment Harry could not think. But then he remembered Bertrand talking as they rode through the countryside. He remembered a convent, one in the direction from which they had come. He said the name aloud.

The Frenchman frowned. "They do not take vows of silence there."

Harry made himself frown and then shrug carelessly, as though the woman's life did not depend on how well he did so. "Perhaps not. This woman, however, does not speak. At least I have never heard her do so."

He held his breath, hoping she would not contradict him. Fortunately she held her tongue. The officer regarded both then bowed to the nun. "My apologies, *ma soeur*. You will understand we must be certain?"

She inclined her head graciously. The officer turned to one of the men and rattled off his orders. "You must go to the convent. Ask if they had such a sister there. How long and where was she from. And ask if she was indeed sent off in the company of this priest."

In moments the soldier was gone, riding away as fast as though there were hounds at his heels. Bitterly

Harry realized he had bought his companion a few days respite at most.

Prudence watched the exchange with growing anger. The man had lied to her. And man he apparently was, not priest. Of all things, he was a soldier! She was furious. At him and at herself, for caring about a liar and a soldier. It went against everything she believed in.

She was even more furious at the claim that she had taken a vow of silence, or at least never spoke. The story he told, she thought, would not have fooled a child. Now she had to listen, helpless as the officer gave his soldier the orders that would inevitably lead to her unmasking. And if she even tried to help, she could only make matters worse by giving the lie to his tale right now.

So Prudence had to listen in silence to the rude jests made by the men. Then he made matters even worse, this false priest. The French officer was talking to his men, giving orders for some to continue their scouting, for others to help him bring the prisoners back to a nearby village. At the sound of Harry's voice, he turned to look at him.

"I think she may be partly deaf," Père Alain, or rather, the English officer, said in a conversational tone, leaning forward toward the Frenchman.

"Deaf?" the Frenchman regarded the mock priest in patent disbelief. "But she nodded when I spoke to her."

"She always does that, no matter what anyone says."

Then it came to Prudence what Père Alain intended. If she were thought to be deaf, the men would lower their guard around her and she might learn something of use or have a better chance to escape. In his own way, he was trying to protect her and for that she was grateful. But she would have to be more careful than ever.

Prudence did what she could to lend support to the story. She regarded the officer with limpid eyes and each time he spoke a series of increasingly absurd things to her, she graciously nodded. She did not understand all the words and that made her pretense even easier.

Eventually he tired of the game and turned back to Père Alain. "It would seem, perhaps, that you are telling the truth. It is a sad thing that the poor creature was placed in your care."

Père Alain shrugged and quirked an eyebrow upward. "I took very good care of her, I assure you. And behaved as if I were indeed the priest I pretended to be."

The officer sighed. "Why did you have to cross my path again, Major Langford? I like you. It is going to make me most upset when my orders come to kill you. Or, worse yet, to have to turn you over to some of Napoleon's men for questioning."

So he was Major Langford? Prudence would have to remember it. She could no longer go on thinking of him as Père Alain.

"It is now Colonel Langford. But you will see the nun safe to her convent?"

"*Bien sûre. If* she proves to be who you say she is," the Frenchman replied with a bow.

And that, Prudence thought, meant her doom was sealed, unless she thought of something fast. She must find a way to escape before the soldier returned from the convent.

But that was clearly not going to be easy. They rode, this Colonel Langford and herself, surrounded by the soldiers, the officer riding behind them, his pistol at the ready. Langford joked with the man as they rode.

"I hope your hand is steady and your horse doesn't decide to bolt," he told the officer.

"I am tolerably certain I can manage to control both," the Frenchman replied.

From time to time, the officer would speak to Prudence. She pretended not to hear for he was behind her and she ought not, if she were truly deaf, to even know he had made a sound. Gradually it seemed to her that there was less taunting in the Frenchman's voice, as though perhaps he was coming to believe Père Alain's absurd tale of deafness. She hoped so, for on it might rest whatever slim chance either of them had for escape.

Soon they reached the village. It was evident that a portion of it had been commandeered by soldiers. They were led to the grandest house, which wasn't very grand, perhaps, but bustled with activity.

One of the soldiers helped Prudence from her horse. She pretended to stumble against him. It was no trick to let her face seem pale from fatigue because she was. Indeed, she was very close to fainting and made no protest as the soldier helped her into the house. If she seemed weak enough, perhaps they would not think to search her.

As if from a distance, Prudence heard the officer give his orders. "The nun, we believe she may be deaf. Help her, Madame Salvage."

"Ah, the *pauvre petite*! So young to take her vows. No doubt it is the deafness which made her parents place her with the good sisters. I will help her, *Bien sûre*. She will rest. Eat a little. Sleep. I will keep watch over *la petite,* I assure you."

Prudence was careful to give no sign that she heard or understood anything of what had been said. And indeed the French had been spoken so rapidly that she could not be entirely certain she had heard correctly anyway.

Behind her, Prudence could hear the officer's voice turn harsh as he gave very different orders for the colonel.

Harry would have paced the small interior of his prison had he not been shackled to the bed. But Jean

Louis Dumont was taking no chances. And he had good reason for such caution.

The last time they met, he had also held Harry prisoner. But Harry had escaped and taken him prisoner. It was only when the lines overtook their position that Dumont managed to escape in his turn.

So Harry could not blame Dumont for the precautions he took now, but it was a damnable nuisance anyway. As was the knowledge that the woman upstairs was no doubt equally well guarded, albeit in gentler and more comfortable circumstances than his own.

Indeed, Harry more than half suspected that even if he did manage to escape, if he went looking for Prudence, he would find her to be the bait in a well-laid trap meant just for him. He had to hope that she was as quick-witted as she seemed and would find her own means to escape. She was a deuced nuisance but it was his failure to protect her that rankled almost more than his own capture.

Almost. Because Harry could not forget that Wellington was waiting for the reports that only he could bring. It was that memory that led Harry to fruitlessly tug at the shackles that bound him to the bed.

The prison door opened then and an old woman, the woman they had seen when they entered the house, appeared with a tray of food for him. She chattered as she set it down on the small table by the bed.

"Ah, the *pauvre petite, mon Père*. She sleeps. So tired, that one. Two floors above. She asks for you, I think, in her sleep."

He might have believed her except that Harry could not bring himself to credit the notion that Prudence would ask for him under any circumstances. No, it was a trap. It had to be a trap. Jean Louis Dumont would never allow such information to be given to him so carelessly. There had to be a purpose to it.

Harry made his voice cold and indifferent as he said, "You must be mistaken, Madame, in what you believe

you overheard. I have nothing to do with the nun or
the nun with me, save that we traveled together for a
short space and I used her as my shield."

The old woman crossed herself at these harsh
words. She clucked disapprovingly about priests who
ought to be defrocked. And she bustled away with an
angry sniff.

Harry watched her go. He would not, he dared not,
ask a word about Prudence. Her life might depend on
his apparent indifference.

Upstairs, Prudence woke to the sound of a gun fir-
ing in the street below. Her heart pounded. Had they
shot Père Alain already? Surely not in the middle of
the night? Unless he had tried to escape, a tiny voice
whispered in reply. It might have been like him to
do so.

Her first instinct was to rise from her bed and go
to the window to look. But she could not, she realized.
If she were being watched she did not dare reveal
that she had even heard the shot, much less that she
might care.

No, for so long as she could, Prudence must pretend
to be the deaf nun. And she must also pretend that
she did not know, did not care, who her priest companion might have been. To do anything else would
be to put both their lives at even greater risk than
they already were. So, as difficult as it was, Prudence
made herself close her eyes again and try to go back
to sleep.

At least she did so until it occurred to her that there
was a *prie-dieu* in the room. She could kneel at that,
as if in prayer, and who would dare to call it wrong
or connect it with plans of escape? What would be
more natural for a nun? Or what stranger than to not
see her at her prayers?

Prudence rose from her bed and donned her nun's
habit. She clutched the rosary in her hands and knelt
at the *prie-dieu*. The padding felt well worn under her

knees and her hands rested on the small shelf but it was enough to support her. It felt strange to be doing so, but there was no sham in her prayers for guidance in finding a way to escape, in asking for both her life and the colonel's to be spared.

She listened as well to the footsteps of soldiers in the street below. To footsteps in the house itself. One could not, she realized, hope to slip out unseen as the household slept for it never did. But then Prudence had not thought escape would be easy. Not when she did not even know where Harry was being kept.

Still, there were no more shots fired, no sound of a man's screams to be heard. And when, in her fatigue, Prudence could think of nothing more to listen for, nothing more to try, she crept back to her bed and this time truly did go back to sleep. She never even noticed the face that watched from the barely opened doorway.

Capitaine Jean Louis Dumont heard the reports with a growing sense of frustration. "I know there is something between the two!" he growled. "Every instinct tells me so."

The old woman shrugged. "Me, I saw nothing to tell me so. He did not seem to care. She asked nothing about him. Indeed, she does not speak at all. Nor react when I do so."

"Nonetheless," Capitaine Dumont said with certainty, "there is something there. The question is, are they both spies or is it simply that they are attracted to one another, a man and a woman?"

The old woman gasped and crossed herself. "*Mon dieu!* But he is a priest and she is a nun!"

Dumont glanced at the woman sardonically. "No, he is a spy. An Englishman. She, I do not yet know who or what she may be, but I will find out."

He spoke with a greater certainty than he felt. Dumont could, in truth, only hope that his messengers—one to the convent and one to Paris—would return with due haste and have something, anything, to tell him that would be to the point.

Abruptly he spoke to the old woman again. "Continue to watch. Continue to speak of them, each to the other. Listen. Report anything, anything at all, that you hear."

The old woman looked at him with amusement in her eyes, as if she thought him foolish. But Dumont didn't care. He would find out their secrets, he vowed. One way or another. He only hoped he had time before the entire matter was taken out of his hands by whoever came from Paris.

Chapter 5

The agent from Napoleon, from Paris, stared at both the unmasked priest and at the apparent nun.

"Perhaps I was mistaken in the name of the convent," Harry said with a shrug. "I did not pay a great deal of attention and my French is not so good as I would like."

Capitaine Dumont smiled a thin, mean smile. "I see. I have sent my man back out again. This time with instructions to ask at other convents nearby. There are not so very many, after all, in this part of France. We will see if any of them know of you. Or had within their walls a nun who did not speak."

Harry did not dare look at Prudence. He could feel her tremble beside him. He felt as if he had failed her and he did not know what to do to make matters right.

The agent stepped closer to Dumont and spoke in his ear. They argued for several minutes, but Harry could overhear nothing and it worried him. Finally the agent won. As had been inevitable, Harry thought with a sour smile. He was not surprised when Dumont snapped at him. It must rankle to be overborne by a bureaucrat from Paris.

"You will both leave with Monsieur Gilbert within the hour. And may God have mercy on your souls."

Harry looked at Prudence and drew in a deep breath. He willed her to look at him and when she did he said, "I am sorry, *ma soeur*."

Monsieur Gilbert pounced. He looked at Harry and

tilted his head to one side. His voice was soft and silky as he said, "I thought you said she is deaf?"

Harry shrugged. "She is. But just because she cannot hear or understand does not excuse me from the need to apologize to her for the situation in which she finds herself because of me."

Gilbert bowed, conceding the point. Prudence remained impassive, as though she truly were deaf, truly did not know they had been talking about her. She even kept her head bowed, as though she were the meek creature she seemed, instead of the termagant Harry knew her to be. He could only hope some of that spirit would return soon so that if the chance to escape presented itself on this journey, she would be ready. And he also hoped she still had the dagger he had given her with which to protect herself before they encountered Dumont and were captured. His own had, of course, been confiscated. It reassured him to believe that if the worst occurred, she might be able to defend herself.

But there was little enough time to think. They were herded into a room together, Harry and Prudence, and left alone. Or so they were meant to think. Harry would have wagered that someone was able to see, able to overhear everything that might occur in this room.

Apparently Prudence thought so as well because she made no attempt to throw off her guise, but rather clutched her rosary and seemed deep in prayer. Only he could hear the murmur of her words as she did so and it took him several moments to realize what she was saying.

Prudence clutched her rosary tightly, her hands folded as if in prayer. But she was far more aware of the dagger hidden beneath her robe. If there were a way, she should give it back to the colonel, for that would be far more to the purpose and more likely, she thought, to do them some good.

No more than the colonel did she trust the two

Frenchman. Or the way they had apparently been left alone together. Perhaps, she thought, there might be a way to fool whoever might be watching or listening?

Slowly Prudence began to murmur, her head bowed. Let anyone watching think she was praying. Only the colonel was close enough to hear more than a droning cadence that must have sounded very much like prayer.

"We are not really alone are we? They are trying to catch us in a lie, aren't they?"

Prudence had to repeat these two sentences several times before she saw the colonel's body suddenly stiffen. He half turned away from her, but she knew he had heard her. So she went on.

"We must find a way to escape before we reach Paris I presume. Otherwise we are both done for, are we not?"

Colonel Langford rubbed the back of his neck and managed to nod as he did so. Prudence suppressed the tiny spark of triumph she felt. Surely such optimism was premature? Even with this understanding between them, it would not be easy to find an opportunity to escape. But still the small communication between them comforted Prudence in a way she could not have explained.

Apparently Colonel Langford also felt there was nothing more to be said for abruptly he looked at her, appeared to snort with disgust, and then put as much distance between them as possible. Prudence pretended not to notice, though she wanted to smile at his attempts to fool their captors. Somehow she did not think they were truly that naive.

A moment later the door opened and they were both taken out of the room to mount their mules. The soldiers, she noted with resignation, had horses. They clearly wished to be certain that neither she nor the colonel could possibly outrun them. His hands were bound behind him, at least hers were left free.

It was not a pleasant journey. Aside from the jests of the soldiers about her person, the agent from Paris had apparently decided to see if he could either prod her into betraying herself or Colonel Langford into coming to her defense. His taunts became increasingly coarse. And though she knew it wisest that she pretend not to notice, not to care, it was not easy.

And when they stopped for the night, matters became worse. Apparently Monsieur Gilbert decided that coarse insults were not enough. He insisted on helping Prudence down from her mule and leaned over her as he said, with a leer, "I wonder how much woman there might be under that habit."

Colonel Langford came instantly to her defense. "She is a nun!" he protested.

Monsieur Gilbert shrugged. "Me, I do not care. All the better if I am her first."

"Don't you care how she will feel?"

Gilbert paused long enough to turn and smile at the colonel. It was a very unpleasant smile. "Have you not realized yet? I will enjoy it all the more for her fear."

"The church! It will come after you!"

Again that smile. "She cannot speak. You have said so yourself. And even if she had a tongue, well," Gilbert shrugged. "Who is to say she will reach Paris alive?"

He turned back to Prudence and stroked the side of her cheek, even as his other hand held her arm in an iron grip. "Of course," he said softly, his breath warm and fetid on her cheek, "you may persuade me to keep you with me as long as you can please me."

And then he reached to tear at her clothing. Colonel Langford spoke from behind them, his voice even more desperate than before. "Wait! There is something I must tell you," he said. "Something more important than the nun. My father was the late Lord Darton."

Monsieur Gilbert paused, puzzled. "So?"

"Lord Darton," Colonel Langford repeated with significance.

"I still do not understand," Monsieur Gilbert said impatiently, "nor do I care."

He started to reach for Prudence again and she shrank away. Again the colonel spoke.

In a voice that was soft as silk and very dangerous, he said, "You should care. My father was in correspondence with Bonaparte."

That stopped Gilbert. He looked at the colonel. He blinked. He stood very still as he patently searched his memory. Finally he shook his head.

"I do not know of any such correspondence. Are you certain?"

"It is why I am in France," Colonel Langford replied, his voice as silky as before and this time pregnant with unspoken meaning.

"This correspondence, of what was it about?"

Prudence watched with fascination as the colonel paused, looking for all the world as though he were searching his memory now. Then he spoke of things that made no sense to her but apparently had meaning to both men.

Gilbert's eyes grew wide, he uttered a blistering oath, then he strode over to where the colonel stood and shoved him over.

With his face mottled by rage, Monsieur Gilbert snarled. "So it was your father who stole that letter! Do you know how much trouble that cost us? You thought to help your cause? Well now I tell you it is a thousand times worse!"

Talk of a letter meant nothing to Prudence. Her concern, her attention, was all for the colonel. He did not try to argue. Or get up. Instead he lay very still on the ground and Prudence was grateful for his restraint. Monsieur Gilbert looked to be in a murderous rage and she did not think she could bear it if he hurt Colonel Langford any further.

After a moment, Gilbert regained his self-control. He turned away from the colonel with only one more kick to the fallen man. He drew in a deep breath and

started toward Prudence. There was a look in his eyes
that terrified her. He had said he would keep her alive
only as long as she pleased him. She believed him.

With a shudder, Prudence realized that she was not
likely to survive the night. She drew in a deep breath
and made her decision. She might have been raised
to believe in the sanctity of life, but no one had ever
said she must be a martyr.

Gilbert moved closer. He repeated his words of before. "Now," he said, "let us see how much woman is
beneath that habit."

Prudence had taken advantage of the altercation between Colonel Langford and Gilbert to move away
from the mule and now she took a step backward,
forcing Gilbert to follow. He reached out and pulled
her to him, but not before she had him at the edge
of the clearing.

For an instant she stiffened, then she forced herself
to melt against the man. There was no other way to
carry out the decision she had made. Prudence offered
no protest when Gilbert grabbed her breast or thrust
his tongue inside her mouth. Instead she felt for the
dagger hidden beneath her robes.

When she felt his grasp lessen just a trifle, Prudence
pulled free and tugged at his hand as though to pull
him deeper into the woods. Gilbert gave a tiny crow
of triumph and followed willingly.

He never even suspected when Prudence reached
beneath her robes and retrieved the dagger. She
stabbed Gilbert through the heart. At least she hoped
it was the heart. In any event, he dropped and she
moved quickly away, shaking, and was violently ill.

This was not how she had been raised to behave.
This betrayed every principle she had ever been
taught. But she also remembered the feel of his hands
on her, the sight of him kicking Colonel Langford as
he lay on the ground.

Prudence swallowed hard. She had already betrayed
her principles once and she was about to do it again,

if that was what it took to rescue herself and the colonel. Still shaking, Prudence reached forward to retrieve the knife from the dead Frenchman, but it would not pull free. Instead, she armed herself with a heavy branch and crept back to the clearing where Langford lay.

As she hoped, the soldiers were occupied in speculating about what she and Monsieur Gilbert might be doing. She scarcely spared a glance for the colonel who wisely lay on the ground where the Frenchman had left him. He was, she noted with relief, close to the edge of the woods.

He was the first to see her and when she held a finger to her lips he nodded his understanding. She backed away, out of sight, to consider her options. Perhaps there was a way to help him escape without hurting anyone else?

But the colonel didn't wait for her to decide. Instead he called out softly to the guards.

"I must relieve myself," he said.

He had to say it more than once. They grumbled and made coarse jests but finally the largest one was delegated to accompany Colonel Langford into the woods. Prudence was careful to stay close but out of sight and she heard the soldier agree to free the colonel's hands to allow him to undo his pants rather than do that task for him.

Apparently whatever Langford had planned, he carried out swiftly for in moments the colonel was by her side. "What happened to Monsieur Gilbert?" he asked.

"The dagger you gave me," Prudence said, unable to tell him more. "What happened to the soldier?"

"I had my fists."

Prudence closed her eyes in relief. So he had not killed the man! But she knew they were not safe yet. She opened her eyes and asked, "What shall we do about the others?"

"Wait here."

Before she could ask what he meant to do, he was

gone. A few minutes later the other three guards disappeared, one by one. Shortly after that, Colonel Langford reappeared by her side.

"Come," he said. "We'll take two horses and scatter the rest. We'll have to ride hard and go as far as we can before morning. If we are lucky, no one will find these men for a while and they will not soon wake up. But we must not count on that."

Prudence was not so foolish as to argue. Except that she did say, "Would any of the uniforms fit me? I feel far too conspicuous dressed as a nun."

Colonel Langford considered the matter, then nodded. "Perhaps it would be best. If we are caught you could pretend you had captured me and escape at your first chance. We'll take one uniform now and find new clothes for both of us when we are some distance away. The more we change, the more likely we are to confound any pursuit. But bring your habit as well. Let them wonder whether to look for a nun and a soldier or a priest and a soldier or a priest and a nun. The more confusion the better."

It only took Prudence moments to change once Colonel Langford brought her the uniform. She was as conscious of the need to hurry as he was. He dragged the boy whose uniform they took farther from the rest.

And then they were on their way, riding hard through the night. Only when they had put some distance between themselves and the clearing did Prudence react. She began to shake. But when Colonel Langford asked her if she wished to stop for a moment, she refused.

"I've no wish to be caught again," she answered tartly.

He nodded, though he continued to cast worried looks in her direction as though he felt he could not afford to have her collapse on him. And she didn't. Instead she rallied to confront him.

"So you are English. And a soldier. What were you doing in France?" she asked.

The colonel sighed. No doubt he would have preferred it if he had never had to tell her anything. "You may as well tell me," she persisted. "If we are caught again, I cannot think it likely either of us will survive anyway."

He hesitated, then nodded. "Perhaps it would be as well if you do know," he said. "If something happens to me, I shall have to hope that you can reach Spain on your own. And if you do, perhaps you could give the information I carry to Wellington."

"No!"

Her response was automatic. Instinctive. He stiffened. "You do not understand," Colonel Langford said impatiently. "This is not a mere whim. It is a matter of utmost importance for Wellington to know what the French are doing. It is a matter of saving lives."

"I still cannot do it," she replied, holding herself stiff as well.

He tried to be patient. She could see it in the expressions that crossed his face. Finally he said, "Why not?"

"It is against everything I believe," Prudence replied, trying to explain. "I do not believe in war and I will not help to carry it out."

Colonel Langford gaped at her as though he thought her mad. "And yet," he said, sarcasm evident in his voice, "you did not hesitate to kill Gilbert back there."

She turned her face away. Even in the darkness, Prudence could feel her color rise. In a voice that betrayed her mortification she said, "Do not remind me of my shame. I am not proud of what I did. It betrays every principle with which I have been raised."

His voice betrayed his bafflement. "But our lives may have been at stake," he protested. "And your honor most certainly was!"

"I do not quarrel with the need," Prudence said,

tilting her chin upward in defiance. "But neither can I bring myself to rejoice that I was able to do so."

Colonel Langford spoke evenly, patently choosing his words with care. "I did not suggest you should. But as a soldier, I know that I would no doubt be dead by now if that was how I looked at things."

"And that is precisely why I do not like soldiers," she replied, her voice betraying the depth of her emotion.

There was, Prudence thought, no answer Colonel Langford could give to that and he did not even try. Instead, he said, in a surprisingly quiet voice, "Even this soldier?"

Perhaps it was the wounded boy she heard in his voice. Perhaps it was the reminder, so recent, that there was less difference between them than she might once have thought. Whatever the reason, she reached out and squeezed his hand in unspoken reassurance.

Colonel Langford sat very still and, for a moment, Prudence feared that she had gone too far.

Harry stared at her, far too conscious of the feel of her hand over his, the sound of her soft silvery voice in the night. Thank God there was no one close enough to hear, for if there were there would be no hiding the fact that Miss Prudence Marland was a woman.

The wind ruffled her short hair and he wanted to run his fingers through that as well. But it was all insanity. He must get her to Spain, where she would be safe, and then return on his own to finish his mission. How could her uncle have been so irresponsible as to let her embark on such a madcap mission?

And yet, Harry had to admit that had he been in the poor man's place, he would not have known how to stop her. But he would, he thought with a desperation he did not dare explore, find a way to keep her safe now that she was in his care. It did not matter that she despised soldiers. Whatever her feelings, his duty remained the same: to keep her safe.

Abruptly Miss Marland drew back. Her voice was a trifle shaky as she laughed and said, "Can you imagine how strange we should look if anyone were to see us? A priest and soldier holding hands?"

He was grateful for her jesting. He tried to match her tone. "You are right, of course. We had best be more discreet or we shall find ourselves in trouble, rather quickly."

They rode on in a companionable silence for a while. At last Harry said, "Your uncle. How do you come to be in his care instead of with your parents?"

She looked away and it was some moments before she answered. "My parents died when I was a child. My uncle was the only person who could or would take me in and he has been posted more places as a diplomat since then than I can recall. The latest was Morocco. You wonder that my spoken French is so poor, but truly that was very useful. Things were said in my presence that would not have been said had they known how well I understood. And besides, it seemed far more useful to learn Berber, so that was where I concentrated my efforts."

It sounded like an appalling existence to Harry and he said something of the sort aloud. Immediately she rounded on him and her voice was fierce with anger as she said, "Don't! Don't you dare speak to me like that—with kindness and sympathy! Especially not now, when I have done what I have done! I can bear anything else except either of those!"

He stared at her and then burst into laughter. He knew it was a mistake, because she was already stiff with anger, but he could not help himself. He reached out a finger to flick the side of her cheek.

"I am sorry, *ma petite,* but it is absurd," Harry said, his voice as gentle as he could make it. "Not treat you with kindness? What then am I to do? Treat you with cruelty? I tell you now I will not do it."

"N-no," she conceded. "Of course I don't wish you to do that!" she paused and he could see her drawing in a deep breath, trying to calm herself. "I only meant that when one is accustomed to being strong and on one's own, sympathy and kindness . . ."

Her voice trailed off. "Oh, to the devil with it!" she exclaimed. "I am tired and subject to megrims and you ought not to pay attention to anything I say."

He smiled wryly. He could not help himself, now, either. "I understand," he said. "For I am very much like that myself, I think. To have someone speak with sympathy seems to imply some lack in oneself. And if one has steeled oneself to the vagaries of a cruel world, well, it can be painful to be reminded that it need not have been that way."

She turned and looked at him and this time she was smiling, though her eyes shimmered with what looked suspiciously like unshed tears.

"Precisely," she said. "You do understand."

His voice was still gentle as he told her, "I understand. I have also come to know however, that genuine kindness and sympathy are commodities more precious than almost any other. And however painful they may be, they are also what, in our hearts, we crave."

She was silent a long moment and then she nodded. "So we do," she agreed.

"So," he said briskly, taking a deep breath of his own, "tell me about some of your uncle's postings." When she hesitated, an imp of mischief made him add, "Please, Miss Marland? After all, it will help to keep us awake!"

She made a most unladylike, and unsoldierly like, gesture with her tongue. But when she began to speak, he could hear that the constraint between them was gone and he was very grateful. Indeed, for the first time since it had begun, Harry began to feel this journey might not prove such a sad trial after all.

Chapter 6

They rode long and hard, only stopping very briefly to eat the food he had brought with them from the French camp. They did not truly rest until after sundown the next day. Neither Prudence nor Harry spoke of their discomfort. Not when their lives were at stake.

Harry looked for and found a barn far enough from the house to which it belonged for anyone to notice. "At least they won't," he told Prudence, "if we are gone before daylight."

She did not protest but merely nodded.

"We don't dare risk a fire," he said, "so you'd best sit close to me. We can keep each other warm."

Harry judged it a measure of the shock in which she still found herself that Miss Marland did not protest. Indeed, she had said very little since they first escaped and it worried him. He suspected it had to do with the Frenchman she had killed. Given how hard she had fought against the notion of carrying a knife, it must be haunting her now.

He had seen this kind of reaction before, in the youngest of the recruits, when they did what had to be done in war. He'd always taken the time to speak a word or two to such lads. Now he wondered if there were any way to ease Miss Marland's guilt, or whether she blamed him because he had been the one to give her the knife.

But he couldn't let his fear stop him from trying to help her. So when they had eaten he gently drew her into his arms. Harry thought she was too distressed to protest. Instead she clung to him and started shaking. Tears rolled down her cheeks as he instinctively rocked her, wanting to make matters better and not knowing how.

Eventually she stopped crying but still she did not pull away. Harry wasn't even sure she realized where she was. But she did because her voice came small against his chest.

"How do you do it? How do you live with yourself after you do what you must as a soldier? How can you love killing?"

Gently Harry stroked her hair. "I do not love killing. Neither does almost any soldier I know. Indeed, I think it would be true to say that most of us hate killing. But we do it, I do it when I must, because I know that if I did not, then I would die and so would others. I do it because it is my responsibility to protect the lives of the men under my command, as much as I can. I do it because I believe in honor and because I believe it is my duty to help keep those at home, to keep my family safe. Because someone must."

"You are an odd sort of soldier," she sniffed.

In spite of himself, and even though she could not see it, Harry smiled. "I am not so unique as you might think," he said.

And then she truly surprised him. "Tell me about your family," she said.

"What?"

"Tell me about your family. I have told you about mine."

Bewildered, he stared down at her. How had they gone from talking about death, albeit admittedly in a cloaked way, to talking about his family?

Miss Marland lifted her head to look at him. "You say you do what you do for their sake. I want to understand why. I want to understand them. I want to understand what would make you risk your life for theirs."

He nodded. That he could understand. "I have three brothers. The oldest is George, Lord Darton. A very estimable fellow. He is married to Athenia and they have several children. Four at last count, I think. I am the second oldest. Next comes Philip. He is a barrister, much to my brother George's dismay. And his wife, Emily, is something of a reformer. Then comes James. He seems to be a wastrel but it is only a facade. He invents things. He married a lady named Juliet. They are remarkably well suited. Both Juliet and Emily were in an interesting condition, the last that I heard. And then there is Sir Thomas Levenger and his wife. He stood as something of a second father to us after my parents died some ten years ago. He also is a barrister and Philip's mentor."

"How did your parents die?" Miss Marland asked, tucking her hand into his, though whether for his comfort or hers, Harry could not have said.

It took Harry a moment to find his voice. "Their carriage overturned. My father was a reformer. He was on his way to a meeting with my mother. I must suppose he was driving recklessly. They were killed at once, I am told."

Now she squeezed his hand and there was no mistaking her wish to comfort him. "So we have that in common," she said. "We both lost our parents years ago."

It was his turn to hold her tight and to feel a little of the old pain ease within his heart. "So we do," he agreed, his voice rough with emotion.

She was quiet for several moments, apparently turning over what he had said in her mind for when she did speak it was very much to the point.

"So your father tried to protect others. The common folk. And in your own way you are trying to do the same. By becoming a soldier."

"No!" the protest was instinctive. "I became a soldier to redeem the family honor!"

She looked at him, puzzlement patent in her eyes.

"But what do you mean?" she asked. "Was it not an honorable thing, to wish to help others?"

"Not in the eyes of the *ton*," Harry answered bitterly. "They gave my parents the cut direct more times than I can count. We were, all of us, ostracized for years for his actions and words."

"How unfair!"

Harry smiled but it was a bitter smile. "They did not think so."

"Well I do."

The smile became a little more genuine at the sound of the indignation in her voice. "Well, perhaps a little," he allowed. "But the point is, I wished to prove myself by becoming a soldier. I wanted to show that at least one Langford could help preserve our country, rather than try to destroy it."

Miss Marland shook her head, impatiently it seemed to Harry, but she did not answer that point. Instead she seemed to go off on a tangent. "And I was raised to believe that soldiers and war were anathema to truly being civilized. It is a wonder any of us ever learn to get along with others!"

Harry could not help himself, he laughed. She glared at him and he attempted an apology. "I am sorry, it is just that you have such a novel way of looking at the world. It is vastly . . ." he paused to choose his word, "refreshing."

She seemed a trifle mollified by that. But Miss Marland also seemed to become abruptly aware of where she was and eased herself off his lap. With an attempt at dignity she could not quite maintain, she asked, "Where do we go next?"

There was, there could be, only one answer. However little he liked it, he had to get her there. He had to keep her safe. "Spain."

He expected a protest but she only swallowed hard and nodded. Still, after a moment, she did ask, "And after? After you see me safely to British lines? Will you come back here? To France? To continue your mission?"

He could not lie to her. "Yes."

"I see. It will be dangerous."

"Yes. Doubly so after our encounter with Jean Louis Dumont."

Miss Marland nodded again. And swallowed. As though she had been trained not to protest even those things she most disliked. And though it was surely none of her affair what he did, Harry felt his heart go out to her as she tried so hard not to voice her worry, her disapproval, her wish to change his mind.

Impulsively, he reached out and took her hand in his. Absently he stroked the back of it with his thumb. "I will be careful," he said.

Miss Marland nodded again.

"This is something that is vitally important that I do."

She nodded once more.

"I will come back safely."

Now she looked at him. "You cannot know that! Not for certain!"

Her cry was a protest and a plea all wrapped up in one. And again he could not lie to her.

"No, I cannot," he agreed. "But I will do my best."

This time she did not nod but merely swallowed hard and a single tear trickled down her cheek. He wiped it away with his other hand.

"I will get you to safety first," he promised.

"I would rather you did not go into danger yourself," she protested. "Cannot someone else do it?"

Harry shook his head. All he could say, in a rough, implacable voice, was, "No."

Unfortunately for Harry's plans, he found it was not possible to travel directly south to Spain. There were too many patrols on the roads watching for them. After one such narrow escape, Harry turned eastward.

That evening he explained to Miss Marland the change in his plans.

"We shall have to stay in France for a while," he said, not troubling to hide the frustration he felt. "But not dressed as we are. I have spied a gypsy camp a mile or so back. I propose to go there and trade for some of their clothes."

"Am I to be a boy or a girl, this time?" Miss Marland asked, with a cool composure he could not help but admire.

"A boy, I think, if the clothes will sufficiently hide your person. We shall pass as brothers."

"We don't look very much alike," she objected.

Harry shrugged. "We can't pass for full gypsies anyway so I thought we would claim to have a gypsy mother but different fathers. That should explain the differences between us. But in any event, we must both dress as men. The French will be looking for a man and a woman."

"We could both dress as women," Miss Marland suggested, a smile twitching at her lips.

Harry glared at her but she simply smiled back. "No," he said curtly. Then, at the question implicit in her raised eyebrows he added, "Two women traveling alone would likely not be safe. Particularly from soldiers. We would be unmasked at the first encounter."

That sobered her and she made no further objection. The gypsies proved willing to trade clothes. The soldier's uniform, in particular, seemed to interest them. It was only when they were well away from the gypsy camp, however, that Miss Marland produced yet another surprise. She brought out a bag of brown powder.

"What is that?" Harry asked warily.

"Ground walnuts. It will darken our skin. It is what I used when I masqueraded as a Moroccan prince," she explained.

Harry did not ask, was not even certain he truly wished to know, where she had learned such a trick.

He was too grateful for the powder to argue. Once they were disguised, he regarded her with approval.

"Your apparent gypsy background should serve as sufficient explanation," he said, "for the oddity of your French."

She nodded. "What shall we call one another? I cannot call you Colonel Langford nor Père Alain. It would not be safe. Nor can you call me Miss Marland. We should give ourselves away at once."

Harry nodded. "Agreed. It should be something familiar or similar to our own names so that we remember to answer to them. We can claim to be named after our French fathers. I shall be Alain, since that is the name I have been using as a priest, and you shall be what? Pruet?"

She considered it a moment, then nodded. "Yes, I can learn to answer to that."

"Good. Our lives may depend upon it. Now I think we are ready."

"Ready for what?" she asked doubtfully.

Harry drew in a breath. This was the difficult part. He did not think she would like what he had to say. "I still have a mission to perform. We cannot continue to avoid towns, for that is where I must go to do what I am here to do."

She stared at him and he thought she meant to protest. But, once again, she surprised him. Abruptly she shook her head. Her voice was brisk as she said, "It will not do. Not as we are. I may pass as a young boy but you, you are strong and will be seized into the military by the first commander who catches sight of such an able bodied man who is not in the army."

She was right, of course. His status as gypsy would not protect him in such a case and Harry was angry at himself for not thinking of it first.

"Your suggestion?" he asked in a tight voice.

She tapped a finger against her teeth, then she grinned. "Take off the jacket," she ordered. "And the shirt."

He blinked at her, but did as he was told. The moment his chest was bare, she took the spare rope the gypsies had given her to hold up her trousers and used it to tie his arm close to his body. Then she helped him put the shirt and jacket on over it. Finally she stepped back and observed him from head to toe.

"Yes. It will do," she said. "The clothes are loose enough to hide everything. You look as though you have already lost an arm in the fighting and no one will think twice that you go from town to town begging."

Despite himself, Harry grinned. "You make a formidable ally," he said. "But I think you are mistaken about yourself. I am not certain you look young enough to be safe."

"We cannot both pretend to have lost an arm," she countered. "What do you suggest I do?"

He had already thought about that. He did not think she would like his suggestion but he was not certain what else to do. "I think," he said carefully, "we should give out that you were an early baby and never quite right in the head."

At her look of outrage he held up a hand and explained, "We meant for me to do most of the talking anyway, didn't we? This will explain why you only sit and listen. And you may well overhear things that would not be said in front of you if they thought you had all your wits."

"I cannot like being part of this," she said in a troubled voice.

He put a hand over hers. "I must depend on you to listen for danger to us. I shall not ask you to do more than that, if it goes against your conscience. But what I do will, I hope, save lives."

She did not look entirely content, but neither did she protest further. And so they began their odd adventure. Over the next month, as Harry continued to try to lead them closer and closer to Spain, they learned a great deal.

Sometimes at night they would talk it over. Miss Marland, Harry discovered, had a quick mind and a fair amount of common sense. Still he wished she were safe in Spain or, better yet, back in England.

Chapter 7

One evening they risked building a fire in a cave some distance from the nearest town. As they sat there, after eating, Miss Marland asked Harry again about his family.

He hesitated, then shrugged. "What do you wish to know?" he asked.

"You spoke of them all with such affection," she said, resting her chin on her knees, arms clasped around them, "and it has been on my mind, ever since. I have never felt, you see, that I had a family. Certainly not one like yours. Indeed, there were times when my uncle seemed to scarcely remember my existence."

"That much is evident!" Harry exclaimed. "For how else could you have ended up aboard a ship, dressed as a foreign prince and headed for Spain?"

Miss Marland sighed and leaned closer to the fire. "For all his experience," she said, neatly evading the question, "I think there are times my uncle does not understand his work very well."

"And you do?"

She sighed again. "Yes, as arrogant as I may sound, I do. And going to Spain was part of it. It was a foolish thing to attempt, I know, but my uncle was being sent to join Stewart in Prussia. He could not seem to understand that in order to negotiate properly he needed to know what was really going on in Spain."

She paused and looked at Harry. Her eyes were

earnest as she said, "You must understand that we were receiving the most conflicting reports and how could one negotiate from that? So when my uncle would not agree to go to Spain first, I said that I would and then join him with the news of what I learned."

Miss Marland paused, then added dryly, "I have masqueraded as a boy before. The last place my uncle was posted was Tangiers, to the court of Moulay Soulaiman. It would not have been safe for me to go out and about if I hadn't been dressed as you saw me. And as slender as I am, it was easy to pass as a boy. No one ever seemed to guess the truth."

Harry tried to imagine what such an existence must have been like for her. "Do you prefer to dress as a man, then, to wearing skirts?" he asked at last.

She laughed and shook her head. "No. What I like best is to be in my skirts. Especially my satin or velvet skirts, with pearls at my ears and throat. For then men hang on my words and answer every question I ask them and I can lead them wherever I wish."

It was said unself-consciously, as though it were the simple truth and Harry supposed it was. He felt jealousy at all the men who had ever seen her that way and a pang of loss at the thought that perhaps he never would.

"You are very quiet," Miss Marland said, her own voice sober. "Have I shocked you, then?"

Harry reached out and put a hand over hers. Perhaps it was the moonlight, perhaps it was all the time they had spent together so far. But in the end he shook his head and told her the truth.

"No. I was simply wishing I could see you like that someday."

Her brown eyes were bright and large and shining as she whispered back, "Perhaps some day you will."

He lifted his hand, then, to touch the side of her cheek. Unconsciously she tilted up her chin and her lashes trembled, but her gaze met his, completely unafraid. Harry leaned forward, slowly, to give Miss

Marland time to withdraw if she wished. Instead she met him halfway.

He had feared he would find that she was accustomed to kisses, this odd sprite before him. But her lips trembled under his and her hand was tentative as she reached up to grasp his shoulder for support.

There was an innocence about her that she could not hide and it was then that Harry knew however irregular her upbringing may have been, the essential Miss Marland was as untouched as that of any English miss at her first coming out ball.

When they broke apart, her eyes were wide and luminous. She gulped at the night air, for she found it hard to breathe, and looked at him as though not certain whether to be frightened or to ask for more.

"I think," Harry said, in a voice that was none too steady, "that we had best not do that very often or we shall surely scandalize the countryside."

Miss Marland gave a shaky laugh. "We have said that before and seem to forget it anew each time."

Now Harry gulped at the night air as he drew back, trying to put some distance between them. He tried for lightness in his voice but missed. "So we do. We shall just have to keep reminding ourselves then. Or make our way back to Spain a bit faster so that I can send you back to your uncle."

She looked away, staring into the fire, and he could feel the hurt his words had caused her. "You are so eager to be rid of me, then?" she asked, not looking at him.

"I—"

He found that he could not lie to Miss Marland, though it would have been wiser. He could not tell her the words that would drive her away. Nor could he tell her how he truly felt for that would have been worse. For both of them. In the end he said nothing.

"Never mind," she said, her face still hidden from him. "I shall not press you, for I already have my answer. You never wished to be saddled with me and

I cannot say that in your place I would not feel the same."

He watched as she rose from the fire and walked the short distance to where he had laid out her blanket earlier. She rolled herself up in it and Harry sat, fists clenched at his sides. It occurred to him that they had not talked about his family after all. But then it didn't matter. What mattered was what was happening, but should not happen, between them.

As he looked over at her, Harry found himself wishing he had met Miss Marland under different circumstances. Perhaps at a ball in London. Then he might have courted her. But not here, not when she was in his care.

And yet he knew that she wished he would. Indeed, it was the hardest thing he had ever done, not to go to her now and wipe away the tears he knew she was shedding.

Prudence lay curled up in her blanket. It should not hurt so much to know he wanted to be rid of her, but it did. How could she have lost her heart to a man who was wed to the military? After all the years spent in the company of men who were soldiers, assigned to the embassies where her uncle was posted, she should have known the danger of that! She, of all people.

She tried to tell herself that she hated war, hated soldiers with the greatest passion. Except that Prudence could not hate Alain. She could not even think of him by the formal title of Colonel Langford. Not after these weeks together.

And yet, was it not she who had counseled more than one woman never to lose her heart to a uniform? But Prudence hadn't lost her heart to a uniform. She had lost it to a raggedy gypsy priest. She had lost it to a man who understood her fear of kindness and gave it anyway. She had lost it to a man who needed her as much as she needed him, even though he did

not yet know it. She had lost her heart to a man who
might never understand how alone he was.

She ought to walk away, when they reached Spain.
She ought to let Alain send her back to England and
go to join her uncle as planned. But she would not.
That same fierce determination that had sent her
toward Spain would now be enlisted in the cause of
making Colonel Langford give her his heart. And she
had no doubt that in the end she would win. It was
just getting to that point that would be the problem.

Prudence was almost asleep when she heard the
horses whinny. Something had obviously disturbed
them. Apparently Alain heard them too for he stood
and doused the fire, as though ready to go to sleep.

She watched as he lay down on his blanket, laid out
on the far side of the cave from hers, pretending he
had heard nothing. But he moved with a purpose she
had come to recognize. She would have bet he had a
dagger in his hand. And she held herself ready as well.

When Alain had stolen her a uniform, he had stolen
the man's knife too and insisted that she carry it. Now
she silently pulled it out of its hiding place and lay
very still with the knife in her hand, covered by the
blanket. No one would miss her, except perhaps her
uncle in passing, but she was determined that Alain
would make it back to his family safe and sound.

She didn't doubt that he would be appalled at her
presumption if he knew. But Alain had saved her life
and, despite the encounter with Monsieur Gilbert, the
debt was not yet repaid. Prudence always repaid her
debts.

The sound of something moving outside the cave
came closer. Only now it sounded less like it could be
a man. Alain was the first to realize the truth. He rose
from his blanket and came over to hers.

"It is a wild creature," he said. "A bear I think. I
shall try to scare it away. Dousing the fire may have
been a mistake."

He started to go and Prudence reached out a hand

to stop him. "Be careful," she said and even she could hear the fear in her voice.

He quirked that odd smile that had become so dear to her heart. Then he bent forward and dropped a kiss on her forehead as he whispered, "I shall."

Prudence lay still, listening as he moved toward the mouth of the cave and slipped outside. What if he were wrong? She wondered. Or what if Alain were right but instead of being scared away, the creature attacked him?

Even as she asked herself that question she heard the sound of something scrabbling on the stones and then falling. There was a wild keening sound and Prudence flinched.

A shape appeared in the opening of the cave and she gripped her knife tighter, only to drop it with relief and fling her arms around his neck when Alain reappeared at her side.

"I was so afraid you would be hurt!" she sobbed.

In answer, he held her tighter and made soothing sounds even as his hand stroked her hair. Her body seemed wracked with sobs and when, finally, she could pull back, Prudence was grateful for the darkness that hid her blushes.

"I am so very sorry," she said in a small voice that seemed most unlike her own.

"I do not mind," he replied and she could hear both the gentleness and the amusement in his.

"But I mind," she said tartly. "I never cry."

"Never?"

"Well, never like this," she allowed.

He pulled her close again and this time tucked her head beneath his chin. "You have been through a great deal," Alain said with the same gentleness as before, the same gentleness that threatened to totally undo what little hard-won composure she had regained. "It is no wonder you should feel overwhelmed."

"*You* don't," she said accusingly.

He chuckled. "On the contrary, I know the sensation well. But we colonels are schooled never to betray our fears. Nonetheless we have them."

She turned to look up at him. "Truly?"

"Truly."

And then she would have sworn he meant to kiss her. He bent his head closer but abruptly he pulled back and set her down.

"Go to sleep," he ordered and there was neither warmth nor kindness in his voice, only anger.

And yet, Prudence found herself oddly comforted anyway as she fell asleep.

Chapter 8

It was longer than either of them expected before they crossed the mountains into Spain. During all that time, Harry had not let himself touch Miss Marland again. Not even to help her over the stones in a stream or up a difficult path.

Now they were close to English lines, or so he hoped, and it was more important than ever to keep his distance, Harry told himself. But it was almost a physical ache to see her bright smile, her hair shining in the sunlight, or the way her eyes seemed to dance when she laughed.

"Where are we headed?" she asked, coming alongside of him.

Harry frowned. "I am not entirely certain. It has been a long time since I left and I cannot be certain where we will find Wellington."

She nodded.

"You've become almost tame," he teased. "I cannot recall the last time you challenged me."

"Do you complain?"

"Oh, no," he replied with a sober face belied by the twinkle in his eyes. "I like my women to be docile and quiet you know."

She snorted a most unladylike snort of disgust and he chuckled. So, after a moment, did she.

Oh, yes, he thought, he'd been right to stay away from Miss Marland. There was too much magic in her smile, too much danger in those rich brown eyes. Harry's smile faded as he stared at her.

And then her own smile faltered. "Is something wrong?" she asked.

The sound of footsteps nearby and men stepping out of the woods, guns trained on the pair, obviated the need for an answer. With a vast sense of relief, Harry realized the uniforms were English.

"Halt!"

Harry slowly raised his hands to show they were empty and Prudence beside him did the same. "I am Colonel Langford," he said crisply. "Which regiment are you from?"

"Oh, a colonel is it?" one said in disbelief.

"Aye, dressed like that, of course 'e is," another added sardonically.

"And is the lad yer corporal?" a third chimed in.

"I am Colonel Langford," Harry repeated, "and you had best take me to see Wellington at once."

"Oh, it's Wellington 'e wants to see. Right quick, too, I've no doubt," the second man said to the others.

"Come along now," the first said to Harry and Prudence with no little exasperation in his voice. " 'Tain't my job to sort you out, just to bring you in. There's others what'll decide who you see. And when."

Harry shrugged at the men, then looked at Miss Marland and smiled reassuringly. "It shouldn't take long to sort this out," he promised.

She nodded, bravely he thought, though he could see the hint of fear in her eyes. He didn't blame her. Not when no one would believe who they were. If they put her in with other prisoners, her unmasking as a woman would come quickly. But he could not believe it safer to tell these men either. He would have to hope that he knew the officers to whom they were taken.

Prudence had never seen a soldier's camp before. The things that struck her most were the smell and the dirt and the noise. All of it seemed overwhelming and she clung to Alain's side.

The soldiers would have separated them as soon as they reached camp, since Alain had claimed to be an officer and she, so far as they knew, was no one. But he insisted they stay together. He claimed they both had important information for Wellington. It was clear the men doubted this claim, but they did not quite dare to override him without the orders of a superior officer.

Prudence was grateful for Alain's protection. Colonel Langford's protection, she reminded herself. She must become accustomed to thinking of him, of speaking to him, in such formal terms or she would scandalize everyone. And she did not wish to cause him any more trouble than she must.

She did not doubt that Colonel Langford meant to send her back to England as soon as possible. But it was clear that until he could, he would do what he must to make certain she was safe.

She didn't know any of the men they encountered, but she understood negotiations. She understood that Alain was taken aback at how difficult it was proving to reach Wellington. But somehow he managed to persuade the third officer they saw. That man at least seemed to believe Colonel Langford's claim of who he was. Though he didn't know him, the officer agreed to send him on to Wellington.

"The lad can stay here. I'm short of men," the officer said.

"No. He must come with me. He has information Wellington must hear," Alain insisted.

The officer peered closer. "This ragamuffin? Tell me, boy, is this true? Do you know something essential?"

Prudence nodded. Even for the boy she pretended to be her voice was pitched a trifle high to trust it now. And she was painfully aware of how much her hair had grown in the past couple of months tramping about France.

Maybe something in her face showed. Maybe it was

the way he studied her so closely. But suddenly the officer straightened, blinked, and turned to Alain.

"My God!" he whispered. "He's a woman!"

Colonel Langford closed his eyes and opened them again and sighed with resignation. "Yes. She is a woman. We had hoped to keep that secret until I got her safely to Wellington."

"But who is she? And how did she come to be with you, in France?"

Perhaps she should have left it to Alain. He was, after all, remarkably inventive with a story. But Prudence was tired of being spoken of as if she were not there.

"I fell overboard during a storm from the ship I was on and washed ashore where Colonel Langford found me," Prudence said curtly. "Since there was no other way to get me home, the colonel was forced to drag me across France with him. This," she added, gesturing toward her clothes, "seemed the safest disguise."

Now the officer seemed more stunned than ever. "You have a lady's voice," he said in a tone of wonder.

"Well of course I do!" Prudence snapped, too tired to be diplomatic. "My father was a gentleman and my mother a lady and I assure you I was raised to be one as well. I am Miss Marland."

And what there was in her words to cause such a look of distress to cross Alain's face she could not imagine. Nor did she understand the silent message that seemed to pass between the two men.

The officer cleared his throat self-consciously. "Yes, well, er, Colonel Langford we must do something about this. I have no clothing suitable here for a lady."

"Why do anything?" Prudence asked with exasperation. "I am perfectly content to continue my masquerade for the moment. Time enough to find me other clothing after we have seen Wellington. And then, frankly, I shan't care whether it's silk and satin or the veriest peasant skirt someone can find for me."

Again that odd look passed between the two men.

"I shall, of course, handle things directly after we've spoken to Wellington," Colonel Langford said to the officer. "But she is quite correct that we should brook no delay in reaching him."

The officer nodded. "I'll have you on your way within the hour. It's an honor to meet you, Colonel Langford. And, er, most interesting to meet you, too, Miss Marland." He paused as a thought occurred to him. "Perhaps it would be best if you both waited here, out of sight, until the horses are ready and I've a man to take you," he suggested.

Colonel Langford agreed. He seemed at ease. But the moment they were alone, his face settled into bleak lines. Prudence gently touched Alain's arm.

"What's wrong?" she asked.

He hesitated. "I wish," he said at last, "that he had not realized you were a woman."

"Does it matter? Surely people would have learned soon enough."

Again the hesitation. "I had hoped," he said, "that we would find a way to spirit you out of Wellington's camp and back to England with no one the wiser."

"But I don't care. Truly," Prudence said, trying to reassure him.

Colonel Langford grimaced. "Unfortunately," he retorted, "I do. This will not end by affecting you alone."

"Why the devil not?"

But Alain only shook his head and refused to explain. Which was really, Prudence thought, most provoking. Still, she could not force him to talk so she spent the time pacing about the tent. Now that they were here, in Spain, she could not wait to meet the man all of England considered its savior.

The ride was a long one. Not because they had so incredibly far to travel, but because there were patrols every few miles along the way. Or so it seemed. Maybe, Prudence told herself, the journey just seemed a long one because Alain refused to speak with her. Indeed, it became almost easy to think of him as Colonel Langford. He seemed so lost in his own thoughts, so reserved when he responded to her questions, that she began to feel reluctant to intrude.

But then they reached Wellington's headquarters. Instinctively she straightened as they approached the man and she had to suppress the urge to curtsey. That would indeed have drawn all eyes, dressed as she was as a boy.

Wellington greeted the colonel like an old friend and Prudence was surprised to feel a pang of jealousy.

"Colonel Langford! Good God but I am glad to see you again! We'd begun to think you lost. Come, you must tell me everything that happened. And everything you learned."

Wellington started to turn away but Colonel Langford stopped him. "Sir, there is someone you ought to meet. Someone who was of invaluable assistance to me and whose story you will find just as fascinating as mine."

Wellington was curious. He looked at Prudence and frowned. "This boy? Is he French?"

"That sir, is all part of the tale we have to tell you," Alain replied, evading the question neatly. "But in private, I think."

"Very well. In private," Wellington agreed.

In moments they were seated and being served tea. Colonel Langford waited until everyone else had been waved out of the tent by Wellington before he began. And then he told his story, start to finish and omitting, so far as Prudence could tell, absolutely nothing. From time to time one or both men would turn to her and ask questions. She did her best to answer. So amiable was the conversation, that she was lulled into a false sense of security. That was why the words Wellington

spoke, at the end of the hour, came as such a shock
to her.

"You'll marry the girl, of course. As soon as it can
be arranged. Then we'll get her on a boat to England
and your family can take care of her."

Prudence stared at the man, stunned, and waited
for Colonel Langford to contradict Wellington. But he
didn't. Instead he nodded and replied, "I shall write
a letter to send on ahead, warning them, and another
for her to carry with her, in case the first does not
reach home in time."

"Good. I'll speak to the chaplain and there will be
no difficulties, I am certain, about the short notice."

"And I shall find someone to escort her back to
England," Colonel Langford added.

It was too much. Prudence began to get over her
shock and to feel her temper rising. Indeed she did
actually rise to her feet and stare down at both men.

"You are speaking as if I am not even here!" she
protested. "Do I have nothing to say in this?"

They shook their heads. "You were alone, in Colonel Langford's company for weeks, at night, and you
are a well-born lady. There is no alternative but for
the two of you to marry," Wellington said in a reasonable tone.

But Prudence did not wish to be reasonable. "It is
ridiculous!" she said, feeling close to tears. "Colonel
Langford has no desire to marry me! Let me go back
to England disguised as a boy. No one need ever
know."

It was Alain who shook his head. "Too many know.
The man who brought us does. And he will tell others.
No, there is no other way to salvage your reputation.
Or," he added, holding up a hand to forestall her
when she opened her mouth to protest again, "any
other way to salvage mine."

Prudence closed her mouth and sat down. "I don't
like it," she muttered.

Colonel Langford shrugged. "Neither do I," he said

carelessly, "but I, at least, know enough to do my duty."

And why that should push her over the edge into despair was more than Prudence could have said.

Chapter 9

Almost the first person they encountered outside Wellington's headquarters was Colonel Langford's batman. He came running straight toward them. "Colonel 'arry, is it really you? I couldn't believe me ears when I 'eard you was back!"

Harry grinned. "It most certainly is me. How have you been, Wilkins?"

"Worritin' meself sick over you. When you didn't come back arter a month there was them as said you never would," the man mournfully replied. Then, noticing Prudence his eyes narrowed. "A gypsy boy? What's 'e doing 'ere? We don't want no riffraff like that 'ere abouts."

"Er, Wilkins?" Harry said, lowering his voice so that the batman would lower his. "This isn't, er, riffraff. This is Miss Prudence Marland and she is about to become my wife."

Wilkins opened his mouth to speak and shut it again. He stared at Miss Marland, then back at Harry. Finally he looked her straight in the eye and said, bluntly, "I don't like it. I don't like it at all."

And then he stalked away.

Beside Harry, Miss Marland shivered and he tried to give her an encouraging smile. "Wilkins has been with me for some time," he explained. "And therefore thinks himself entitled to say the most outrageous things."

She stared at him. "The most outrageous things,"

she echoed. Then, "Like calling you 'Harry?' Colonel Harry? Not Colonel Alan?"

Harry felt his color rising. He'd forgotten about that. About the fact that he'd never told her his real name. Now he all but stammered as he said, "Well, er, it's Colonel Harry Alan Langford. It seemed safer to use the Alan while I was in France and I thought it would only confuse you if I told you about my other name."

"I see."

Harry knew that edge of ice in her voice. He'd heard it often enough when his brother's wives were mad at his brothers to know what it meant. But truly, what could he do about the matter now?

To his great relief, one of the few respectable women in camp suddenly appeared and said, "I've been asked to show Miss Marland to her quarters and find her something more respectable to wear. If you'll come with me?"

Miss Marland shot Harry a worried look but all he could do was smile and indicate she should go with the woman. Then he set off in the direction Wilkins had gone. His own quarters, wherever they might be, however makeshift, sounded very inviting at the moment.

Two days later Prudence stood in the middle of a small room with a dirt floor and mud walls as the women of the camp helped her dress. How, she asked herself, could she possibly be getting married? And to a man who wanted no such thing? She had not missed the resignation in his face as he agreed with Wellington two days before. Nor his batman's incredulity. No, this was not something Alain, or rather Harry, wanted either.

But like so many others before her, Prudence was discovering just how futile it was to resist Wellington's orders. So now she stood in a poorly fitting dress lent by one of the officer's wives, ready to be led out to where the chaplain was waiting, where they were all waiting, for her to take her vows with Colonel Langford.

She did not doubt he would be there. She knew only too well how highly he valued whatever he perceived to be his duty. Duty! Prudence began to think she hated the word.

It would be different if he cared for her. For she had long since lost her heart to the man she knew as Alain. But to know that he was being forced into a marriage he did not want hurt far too much for her to be complacent.

When would he come to hate her? In a day? Or a month? Or a year? When would he come to berate her for the folly that had led to his finding her on the beach and leading to this grotesque wedding day?

It was no wonder, then, that Prudence found herself fighting back tears even as the few respectable women in the camp crowded around, admiring her. They teased her, but gently, all too aware of the circumstances regarding this marriage. They tried to console her and for their kindness she was very grateful.

Kindness. It was Alain who had taught her to be. able to accept kindness. Alain who had taught her to trust him. She refused to think of him as Harry, at least for today. It was the only thing that might make it possible for her to go through with this charade.

"He's a handsome man," one of the women said, trying to coax a smile out of her.

Prudence shrugged.

"Kind, too. Helped out my James more than once since we've been here."

"Yes, he is kind," Prudence agreed, smiling at her own memories.

"And a good lover, I'll be bound," yet another said, with a saucy grin.

Prudence colored. "I-I have no way to know," she said weakly.

The other women exchanged skeptical glances. They

did not challenge her, but their disbelief was almost a palpable thing in the room. Was this, then, what both Colonel Langford and Wellington had meant? That all the world would assume they had been lovers?

Finally the first woman cleared her throat and said gently, "It's time to go."

The sight of Colonel Langford all dressed up in his regimental uniform almost undid what little composure Prudence had left. He looked such a stranger! So distant and unapproachable. Where was his smile? The teasing twinkle in his eyes she always found so comforting? Who was this man and what would he think of her as his bride?

Had there not been a hand on the small of her back, pushing her forward just then, Prudence would have turned and fled and to the devil with gossip and what the world would say. But as it was, there was nowhere to go, save forward. Prudence felt as thoroughly hemmed in as ever she had when surrounded by French soldiers.

And then he smiled. A tremulous smile, to be sure, one that betrayed his nervousness was as great as hers. But it was still a smile, a welcoming smile, and Prudence answered it with one of her own. Perhaps, she thought, this would not be so bad after all.

But there was no time to wonder. Already the words were being said that would bind them. Words she scarcely heard, though she answered when she should, her own words ringing absurdly loudly in her ears. She took comfort in the steadiness of Colonel Langford's voice and the way he did not hesitate when he slid the ring on her finger.

And when he kissed her at the end, he also whispered in her ear, "It will be all right, I promise."

It was that promise, along with his strong arm around her waist, that got Prudence through the next few hours. Through all the crude but kindly jests. Through all the moments of wondering what would be her wedding night.

And then they were alone, in quarters that had been vacated just for their benefit. And that was more terrifying than anything yet. She could not meet his eyes and she blushed beneath the feel of his steady gaze. But he seemed to understand.

He reached out a hand and tilted up her chin so that she was forced to look at him. "It will be all right, I promise," he said, repeating his words from before.

Prudence swallowed hard and nodded. He tilted his head and smiled at her. In a teasing tone that unaccountably warmed her down to her very toes he said, "Am I so very different than I was, just a few short days ago? You did not find it hard to look at me then."

She swallowed again. Her voice, when it came, seemed a hopeless croak to her. "We were not married then. And you were Alain, not Colonel Harry."

He looked around but there was no place to sit save on the bed. He drew her over to it and she stiffened. But he only pulled her down to sit on his lap and he cradled her close against his chest.

To the top of her head he said, "I know this is hard for you. It is not what I had planned, either. But I will make this as easy as I can for you. You need do as little or as much as you wish with me. And as soon as I can I shall send you home to England, to stay with my family. My family will take care of you until the war is over and I can come and make a home for both of us."

Without even knowing she did so, she slipped a hand into his. In a small voice she scarcely recognized she asked, "Can I not stay with you?"

"It would not be safe."

She considered. Then, drawing in a deep breath she said, "If I cannot stay with you, then I think I should prefer to go to Prussia where at least I might be of assistance to my uncle."

Colonel Langford hesitated but, in the end, his voice was gentle and implacable. "You will go to England."

The tears began to slip down her cheeks and she swiped at them angrily. "I do not cry like this often!" she said fiercely. "I cannot think why I have done so more than once with you."

He turned up her chin and kissed each cheek, then stared into her eyes as he said, "Perhaps it is because with me at last you feel safe to cry?"

She started to shake her head in denial but before she could speak he lowered his face toward hers.

"Come, let us see if I can give your thoughts a different direction," he said. And then he kissed her.

What a kiss it was! Not a gentle kiss but one that held longing and passion and touched her very soul. His tongue plundered her mouth but gave as much as it took, teasing, dancing, inviting her to respond in kind. And God help her, she did!

She even wound her arms around his neck and turned to press herself closer to him. Somehow she went from sitting on his lap to lying under him on the bed. Somehow her fingers found their way to unfasten the buttons of his uniform and his undid her dress. Somehow her skirts were first up around her waist and then lifted over her head, until she was as bare before him as he was with her.

And somehow her fear was gone. She would not have made Harry marry her, but now that he had she meant to be a good wife to him. It was a vow she made silently, fiercely. Loving him would be no hardship and perhaps, one day, he would come to love her too.

Harry held the woman beside him with a sense of wonder in his heart. He had told the truth when he said he had not planned this. But neither did he regret what necessity had driven him to do. He only hoped that it was not too great a hardship for her. But he would, he vowed, find a way so that she did not regret being married to him. There was more than one way to protect a woman and this was his.

She was sleeping and, in her sleep, moved closer so that she lay against his chest, her leg over his. Harry dropped a kiss on the top of her head. He could not help himself. He felt as though fate had given him a most precious gift and he treasured it.

And then their peace was shattered. A fist pounded on the door and a voice called out, "Colonel Langford? Wellington sends his apologies and says to tell you that he requires your presence at once."

Silently Harry cursed. Out loud he called, "I shall be ready in ten minutes."

Then he slipped from the bed even as Prudence stared up at him, her eyes wide. He paused to kiss her and said, "I shall be back as quickly as I can."

She nodded, pulling the blanket up to cover herself as he finished dressing and opened the door. He paused, just before slipping outside, to take one more look at her. Then he pulled it shut tight behind him. Whatever was afoot, it bode ill that Wellington should have disturbed him on his wedding night. It was not the sort of thing the man would do lightly.

He was right. The first thing Wellington said to him, his face drawn, was, "My apologies colonel but we march at dawn. I shall need your assistance planning the road for our attack. I know this must seem importunate, but we have wasted far too much time already. And between your reports and others I have in hand, my path is clear."

With one last regret for his wife alone in the room, Harry turned his attention to the maps in the center of the room. Within minutes he and the other officers were deep in discussion and everything else, even Prudence, was forgotten. Or if not completely forgotten, set aside in the secure knowledge that what he did now was as much for her safety as for anything.

He did spare one moment to hope that one of the few wives would take Prudence under her wing and keep her thoughts occupied during the fighting ahead. Although if he could, he would arrange for her to be sent home at once. If there was to be fighting, he wanted her nowhere near it.

That was why the news, when it came, that there was a ship in port, was so very welcome. Harry gave the necessary orders and prayed that Prudence would obey them.

Chapter 10

Prudence watched the men marching off down the road. In the distance she could barely see Harry, mounted on his horse, riding up and down the lines making certain everything was as it should be. How it hurt to watch him go.

But her hurt turned to anger when, once they were out of sight, a man suddenly appeared by her side. It was, she realized, Wilkins. Harry's batman.

"Time to go, ma'am," he said briskly.

She stared at him, his words making no sense to her. "Go?" she echoed blindly.

"Aye. Colonel 'arry left orders. I'm to take you straightway to port and see you safely off to England. We'd best be going, Ma'am. He got word just afore they marched that there's a boat there wot'll take you back to England. But we'd best move right quick or we'll miss it and I don't wants to be 'anging about port when I'll be needed 'ere."

For a moment, Prudence could only gape at the fellow. Then her temper engaged. She bristled, visibly so for the poor man took a step backward.

"T'weren't my notion!" he protested, holding up a hand. "T'were the colonel's orders. And I've got to obey orders, don't I?"

That gave Prudence pause. "Perhaps you do," she agreed slowly.

The man gave a sigh of relief. "I knew you'd see reason. Now if you'll come this way, Ma'am, we can collect your things and be going."

But Prudence did not budge. Instead she shook her head. "Oh, no," she said. "I am going nowhere."

"But, but you said you understood," he said, patently bewildered. "You said you understand I've got me orders."

"I do understand," she replied sweetly. "You must obey your orders. But I needn't do so. I am not enlisted in the military. I am only the colonel's wife. And I shall do as I choose. And I choose to stay here."

The man's jaw fell open even wider than before. "But what am I to tell the colonel when 'e returns?"

"You needn't say a thing, for I shall tell him all that needs to be said," Prudence replied.

The man must have read the determination in her eyes for he took another step backward. As he did so, she could hear him muttering to himself. "The colonel won't like this. 'E won't like it at all. But 'e must know what she's like. 'E done up and married 'er, after all."

"Precisely," Prudence said, startling the poor fellow, who had not realized she could hear him.

He took to his heels and Prudence turned to the other women, all of whom were watching the exchange with the liveliest interest in their eyes. Suddenly Prudence felt very cold and she shivered.

One of the women, Eleanor, put an arm around her shoulders. "They'll be back before you know it," she said. "And the colonel will be glad, I'll be bound, that you're still here."

Prudence smiled but shook her head. "No, he will not. But I don't care. I shan't go back until I know he is all right. And until he tells me himself that he wishes me to go and why."

Eleanor seemed to approve for she nodded briskly and said, "Well, then, no sense wasting time. Come along with me and I'll show you how you can be of use. We ladies will be tearing strips of cloth to make bandages while we wait. And gathering all the simples we have to help with the doctoring when they bring the wounded back."

In answer to Prudence's unspoken question Eleanor said, "There are always more who need help than hands to help them. You will be needed and welcome if you'll help."

Prudence nodded. She drew in a deep breath. "I'll help," she said.

The hours passed slowly. Too slowly. In the distance they could hear the thunder of cannons. And then the wounded began to trickle in. Eleanor had been right. There were more men than hands to care for them.

It broke her heart to see the wounds but there was no time for pity. Too many needed her. A sip of water here, a bandage wound tight there, a word of comfort when nothing else could be done for a man.

And all through the hours that followed she watched for him. For Colonel Harry Alan Langford. Terrified that he would be the next man she came upon. In the early hours of the morning he was.

His face was drawn with pain, paler than she had ever seen him before. He clutched his leg tightly but blood still seeped out between his fingers. He saw her at almost the same moment she saw him.

"You were supposed to be gone by now," he said, weakly.

"I wouldn't go," she answered tartly. "Now stop complaining and tell me where you are hurt."

"My leg."

Two words. But his eyes told her the truth, that he knew how badly hurt he was and that the pain went far beyond anything physical.

"I'll get a surgeon," she said.

"I'll wait my turn." She would have gone for help anyway but he stopped her with a hand on her arm. "I'll wait my turn," he repeated. "There are too many men wounded worse than I am."

So instead she stayed. Binding up the wound as best she could. And sponging his brow. And when other

men nearby called to her for water to drink or help
with their wounds, she went.

Eventually it was his turn and when Prudence would
have accompanied him into the surgery, she was gently
but firmly turned away. She watched him disappear
until he was completely out of her sight. Then she
turned and went back to the men, working with grim
determination. In the hours that followed, it seemed
she did not have a moment to stop.

She was holding the hand of a soldier who would
not see the dawn when someone came to find her.
"Colonel Langford is asking for you," the orderly said,
sympathy in his clear brown eyes, which were as weary
as her own.

Prudence nodded. She squeezed the hand of the
young soldier one more time and then she went. As
they moved among the men, the orderly talked, his
voice a necessary steadying force. "The surgeon said
to warn you that you must not show any shock at his
condition, ma'am. It will only upset him and that will
make matters worse."

"What is his condition?"

The orderly took a deep breath, ignoring his own
advice as his voice shook when he said, "He may yet
keep the leg. Within the week we will know."

Prudence closed her eyes then opened them again.
She also took a deep breath. "Thank you for the warning. It will make it easier to conceal my feelings when
I see him. What can I do? To help him, I mean. To
improve the chances that he keeps the leg?"

The orderly sighed. "I don't know. We know so
little about why one man will recover and another
develop poison of the blood or tissues. Watch him.
Care for him. Perhaps he will find a way to heal for
your sake."

Prudence nodded her understanding. "I will do what
I can," she promised.

And then they were by Harry's side, where he lay
on a pallet. If his face had been pale and drawn before

it was ten times worse now. "Go away!" he said, at the sight of her.

The orderly started to protest such cavalier treatment of a man's wife. But Prudence gave him no chance. She stepped between the two men and said briskly, "Nonsense! I am told you asked for me. You cannot take the request back now. Just because you are feeling a trifle downcast. We will have you fit again in a trice."

The corners of his mouth turned down in a way that tore at Prudence's heart. Even in the darkest moments of their journey she had never seen him look so grim. She knelt down and took his hand.

"Grip it as tightly as you like," she said softly, "if it will help."

"Nothing will help," he said, trying to push her hand away.

But Prudence would not let go. "I am here. And here I stay. I am, for better or worse, your wife. Whatever you face, we face it together."

"You should go back to England."

Prudence shook her head. "We go together or not at all. You cannot push me aside so easily."

And then, before he could protest any more, she cradled his head against her breast as he had cradled her so often in the past few months. And if he cried, well there was no one else close enough to see. In the morning, if he asked, she would tell him the whiskey they had given him to deaden the pain had taken control. But for now, she wished him whatever comfort he could find, in whatever way it would come.

That was how they fell asleep, the both of them, exhausted beyond what anyone should have to endure. But that was, she thought as she slipped into dreaming, the appalling cost of war.

Harry woke first. For a moment he could not recall where he was or whose breast he rested against. And then the pain in his leg brought him back to the present. With a groan he closed his eyes, trying to will himself back into oblivion. But it was not so easy and he knew it.

Already the men around them were stirring. And there was the orderly with the surgeon making rounds. When they reached him, Harry reluctantly woke Prudence so that she could move out of the surgeon's way. Then he braced himself for the pain that he knew would follow.

It was Prudence, however, who asked the question uppermost in both their minds. And it was to her that the surgeon addressed his answer.

"We must wait and see. I can tell you now, however, colonel, that it is not likely you will sit a horse anytime soon. As to whether it will affect your gait"—the man paused and shrugged—"only time will tell."

"Will I lose the leg?"

In answer, the surgeon only patted his shoulder then moved on. Harry could not help nor hide the bitterness he felt. He looked at Prudence and said, "It seems you made a worse bargain than either of us could have known."

"Do not say so!" she told him fiercely. "I never took you for a coward! I will not let you become one now. No, nor disparage my skills as a healer, either."

"What the devil are you talking about?"

She knelt again by his side, a hand planted on each side of her on the ground. Her body leaned forward, her face only inches from his so that he instinctively pulled back.

"I have lived in many places with my uncle," she said. "And nursed him through bouts of many things. I will not let you lose this leg."

Harry gave a harsh bark of bitter laughter. "You cannot stop it," he said. "An injured leg is nothing like what you have ever encountered before."

He only meant to tell her the truth, to absolve her of blame if she failed. But that wasn't what she heard. Instead she began to cry. "Don't!" she said fiercely.

"Don't take away from me what little hope I have, what little faith, that I can help you. Don't take away what little faith I have in the world that things may sometimes go right. Don't, above all don't push me away."

He reached out a shaky hand to try to dry her face. But his hand was steadier than his voice as he said, "I'm sorry. I didn't mean to make you cry. We shall get through this together, I promise you."

And when she clung to him, he clung right back. It was nonsense, all nonsense, but he could not, would not, take away what little comfort she might find.

Suddenly she pulled free and stood. "I shall be back as soon as I can," she said.

"Wait. Where are you going?" he asked, feeling oddly bereft.

But she didn't answer. Instead she whirled away and in moments was out of his sight. When she was gone, he became aware that he was being watched. Every man within sight seemed to be staring.

He glared at them, but none looked away. One fellow, perhaps braver than the rest, said cheekily, "A right nice wife you've got, Colonel."

In spite of himself, he smiled. "Yes, yes, she is," he agreed.

And then, in spite of the pain, Colonel Harry Langford leaned back on his pallet and thought about just how lucky he was. Tomorrow he might, perhaps, feel again the guilt that he had pushed Prudence into marriage with a man who, so soon after her wedding, might be a cripple. But for today he would simply be grateful for his good fortune.

Chapter 11

Prudence wiped her forehead. Harry was sleeping. And "Harry" he truly had become to her. A man she scarcely knew. A man who had gone out to battle and killed, because that was his duty. A man who came back injured and would not, except for that first night, let her close to his heart. The man she thought of as Alain was gone and it was Harry who was her husband, Harry who needed her now.

She looked over at Wilkins and he nodded at the colonel. "A natural sleep 'e's in and that's good, I'll be thinking."

Prudence nodded. "If he can only keep the leg."

Wilkins growled. " 'E will. The colonel, 'e's a stubborn one 'e is. And you've nursed 'im right well. Everyone says so." He paused, then added, as though against his will, "I didn't like the colonel marrying you. But I were wrong. It's good 'e 'as you."

Now it was Prudence who smiled. "Thank you. Though I'm not so sure the colonel thinks so."

"Aw, 'e just broods. Worritin' over 'is leg 'e is. But 'e'll come around, 'e will."

"I hope so."

There was a sound in the doorway and Prudence looked over her shoulder. Wellington stood there looking at Harry, an expression of both fatigue and disappointment on his face. Quickly she moved away from the bed and to the doorway, not wanting to wake Harry.

"I have arranged for him to be transported back to England," Wellington said, meeting her eyes.

"His leg is recovering," Prudence said hastily. "He will hate being sent away."

The most powerful Englishman in Spain sighed. "I know it. And I have talked with the surgeon every day. But Harry needs the care he can get at home. And even in the best of circumstances the surgeon tells me that Harry will never have full use of his leg again. Not enough to ride a horse in battle. Or fight on foot."

Prudence wanted to deny it, but she could not.

As if he understood, the duke's voice was gentle as he went on, "At home, surrounded by his family, perhaps he may heal more than we expect. If that is so, I shall welcome him back to my staff with the greatest joy. And if not, then he will be surrounded by family when he must come to terms with his fate."

"How soon?" Prudence asked.

"Another few days before he is well enough to travel. By then there will be a ship waiting to take the wounded back to England. I've arranged a cabin for the two of you to share. You will have some privacy, at least."

"Thank you."

Wellington nodded. He turned to go then paused, his eyes steady on Harry's face. "He was one of my best," he said. "I've lost too many of those here in Spain. But we will be moving, and moving fast, in the days ahead, if I've anything to say about the matter. He would never be able to keep up. Not as he is now."

Then, as if noticing Wilkins for the first time, he looked at the man and added, "You'll go with him. He'll want that, I think."

Wilkins didn't argue, he looked too dismayed to be able to find his tongue.

And then Wellington was gone. Prudence turned back to the bed and was surprised to find Harry watching her with his eyes wide open. Instinctively she glanced at the doorway then back at him.

"You are awake?"

"Evidently."

"Why did you not say so? I'm certain Wellington would have liked to have spoken with you."

"I thought," Harry said, not troubling to hide the bitterness in his voice, "I might learn more if the three of you thought me asleep. I was right."

Wilkins edged toward the doorway. "I'll just, er, go and make certain our dinner is cooking."

Neither Prudence nor Harry tried to stop him. Instead, when he was gone and the door shut behind him, Prudence sat down on the edge of the bed. She was careful not to touch Harry.

Picking up the thread of their conversation from before she asked in a brisk, impersonal tone, "And just what do you think you learned by pretending to be asleep that you would not have learned had you admitted to being awake?"

"That we are going back to England. That Wellington thinks I am of no use to him any more."

"Not in your present condition," Prudence agreed in the same brisk voice as before.

"You are no comfort," he said with a frown.

"I don't mean to be. Not when you are awash with self-pity."

He clenched his lips together and Prudence smiled. "You look like a very small boy right now, you know."

That made him open his eyes wide with shock. She could not keep from pushing a wayward lock of hair off his forehead. "I know," she said softly. "But what can we do except make the best of whatever future it is you have? I will repeat your own words back at you: we will go through this together and it will be all right, I promise."

In answer he caught the hand that was stroking his hair and gripped it tight. For a long moment matters hung in the balance. He wanted to shout at her, to ring a peal over her head, to tell her she didn't understand a thing. And Prudence wouldn't have blamed him a bit if he had.

But he didn't. Instead, slowly, he raised her hand to his lips and kissed the back of it. With a shaky laugh he said, "I keep telling you that I have gotten the better end of this marriage bargain but you refuse to believe me. Perhaps now you do?"

Her own voice was husky then as she shook her head and said, "Never."

And when he reached for her she went into his arms willingly. She had known what it was to be a bride for only one night and part of her was impatient to know it again. But she dared not even ask if it would ever be possible again. For that was one of the things the surgeon had warned her might not happen.

As though he read her mind, Harry took one of her hands and guided it where he wished it to be. "One thing I can promise you, at least," he said softly, "is that when I am a little more recovered I shall in truth be your husband once again."

And what there was about that to make her cry, Prudence could not have said, but it did. This time it was Harry who stroked her hair. And she was the one who took comfort from him.

Later, much later, Prudence asked, "Would you like me to write your family for you? To tell them we are coming?"

Harry hesitated then shook his head. "No. That is a task, I think, that I must do myself. If I do not, they will wonder just how ill I am that I cannot write, that I must leave it to someone else."

Prudence nodded. She caught her lower lip between her teeth. "What will they think of me?" she asked.

He looked at her and all the stiffness left his face as he smiled a warm and gentle smile. "They will find you just as exasperating as I do," he teased. "And think you just as much in need of a guard. But they will also take you to their hearts."

"Even Lord and Lady Darton?" Prudence asked skeptically.

"Even my starched up brother and his wife," Harry confirmed. At her skeptical look he added, "It is the truth, I swear it! George is forever telling me that I ought to get myself leg-shackled. How can he object, now that I have done so?"

"In his place, I should," she countered.

Harry laughed and shook his head. "Perhaps just at first. But he will accept you once he sees how respectable you make me appear."

Prudence looked down at her clothes and laughed. "That should be quite a trick! We must make certain, then, that he catches no glimpse of me until I am dressed a little better than this."

"Oh, I don't know," Harry countered, his eyes merry for the first time in days. "If I bring you home looking like this, then Emily and Juliet are certain to take you to their hearts."

"The reformer and the inventor's wives?" Prudence asked, her own voice turning soft now. "From what you have said, I think I shall like them."

"If we are talking of family," Harry said unrepentantly, "perhaps we should speak about your uncle. What is he going to think of me? Bad enough I am a soldier, but now I shall be a crippled one. What is he going to say when he learns we traveled about the countryside unchaperoned for so many weeks? Will he call me to account for that, do you think?"

Prudence grinned. "Why? Do you wish me to play the part of wronged maiden? I do not think my uncle will believe that any man could take advantage of me against my will. He knows me too well, you see, and he would ask why I had not sunk a dagger in your breast if I found you so objectionable."

"What of your pacifist leanings?" Harry asked warily.

"He would say, and has, that there is a point beyond which idealism becomes foolish," Prudence retorted with a lightness she did not feel.

Harry knew she was thinking of the man she had killed in France and he therefore made his voice lighter, more teasing than it might otherwise have been.

"Your uncle sounds like a most sensible man!" he said.

It was a measure of how well Prudence had come to terms with what happened there that she was able to say, her head tilted to one side, "Well, do you know, I think he is. I also think he will be grateful to you. Which reminds me. Now that you no longer need my constant attention, I ought to write to my uncle and tell him the situation here."

"Do you think that wise?" Harry said with some alarm. "Suppose your letter should fall into the wrong hands? It could be a disaster for Wellington and his men."

"I am not such a fool as that!" Prudence said with a snort. "Years ago Uncle and I contrived a code we could use just between us. No one reading my letter will think I am telling him anything other than the news about my marriage to you."

Harry fell back on the bed with a mock groan. "Now I know for certain that my brothers and their wives will absolutely adore you," he said. "You will become a part of their circle without the least effort! But where were you when we could have used your help a year ago?"

"What?" Prudence asked, thoroughly confused.

"Never mind," Harry said, reaching for her. "Who said I no longer need your constant attention?" he demanded with a growl.

Prudence went into his arms again willingly. She did, she thought as she had so many times since her wedding day, like being married after all, even if Harry could not be brought to understand why. But it was the name "Alain" and not Harry, she whispered just before he kissed her. Because in moments like this she could almost believe he was the same man who had kissed her in France.

Harry carefully slid out from beside Prudence and moved to sit at the desk that had been brought into the room for him. He trimmed a quill pen and dipped it into the ink even as he pulled a sheet of paper toward him.

For all his optimistic words to Prudence, he knew that he had better prepare his family, both for his condition and for her existence. The words were surprisingly hard to find. For a tuppence he would have tossed away the paper and trusted to providence and their relief at his sudden reappearance to avoid questions about Prudence's presence beside him.

But he could not do that to her. She had a right to his protection. And to the consideration of his family. Somehow he must make it clear to them that it was the least he would expect.

Harry would have done so even if this strange marriage of his was simply one of duty. But somehow, in the past few days, even if it had begun otherwise, he had lost his heart to Prudence. In France he had known she had courage. Here he saw it demonstrated tenfold. She had not flinched from dealing with wounded and dying men. She had not flinched from the curses they sometimes hurled at her head. She had not flinched from dealing with him, even when he had been at his worst.

This was not how he had planned his life but, in the matter of his marriage at least, Harry had come to feel, these past few days, that he was more fortunate than he could ever have known beforehand. He had come not only to respect Prudence, but to love her with a depth he had not known his heart possessed.

So dipping the quill pen yet once again in the inkwell, Harry began to write. So lost was he in the effort of composing a suitable missive that he forgot, for some moments, the pain in his leg. And that, he thought later, had to be the best sign of all.

Still, until the moment the surgeon pronounced him completely healed, Harry would not be able to let go of the fear in his heart. He had seen too many men he knew lose their legs in battle for him to be complacent.

Chapter 12

The ship rocked beneath their feet, but this crossing
was far different than the last one Prudence had
experienced. No clouds marred the sky today, nor
storms threatened on the horizon. And she was in
skirts, instead of the robes of a Moroccan prince.

She wished Harry would agree to sit. But he insisted
that he stand, with one hand gripping the rail and the
other balancing on his cane, to watch the shore of
England come into sight. Who was she to deny him
that pleasure? And at least Wilkins stood by, just in
case he was needed.

"Colonel?" a voice said from behind them. They
turned to see the captain standing there. "I've arranged for one of my men to carry your things ashore.
He'll help you get them to wherever you may be
staying."

"Thank you."

The captain touched his cap and retreated. Beside
her, Prudence could feel Harry stiffen. Everyone
seemed to treat him that way, these days. With a mixture of deference and discomfort. Polite to his face
but, embarrassed by his injury, eager to be out of his
company as quickly as possible. And Harry patently
took it to heart every time.

All Prudence could think to do was squeeze his arm.
And then he looked down at her gratefully, as he
always did, but the pain was still there, at the back of
his eyes. The surgeon had shown her how to take

care of Harry's injured leg, but how did one heal a man's soul?

England. His home. Always before he had come back to these shores with a sense of purpose, knowing that he was one of those who helped to defend her. But to what did he return now? To what purpose?

Harry sighed. He could feel Prudence at his side and Wilkins nearby, both watching him with concern. But how could he reassure them when he could not even reassure himself?

He gripped the railing tighter. It would be so easy, even now, with his leg injured as it was, to go over the side and sink below the waves. He might have done it but for two things. Men would have put their lives—Wilkins would put his life—at risk trying to save him, and it would cause Prudence pain. Worse, it would leave her without husband and she would have had to face his family alone. He could not do that to her.

No, at least until he put his affairs in order, Harry had to go on. However much he longed for rest. So now he made himself smile and touch her arm and point out to Prudence some of the things they could see. She had traveled so much that perhaps she knew the sights as well as he, but if so she was perfectly willing to pretend she did not. And for that Harry was grateful.

He seemed to feel that way often these days and it was a sensation he did not like. He would far rather have had it the other way around. He wanted to know that he was the one protecting her instead of feeling, at times, as if she was protecting him.

He also wanted, he found, to show Prudence his England. The places he had played as a boy, the factory his brother Philip now owned, the machines his brother James invented. And he wanted to show her off as well. A smile lit his face at the thought of dancing with her at Almack's.

But there would be no dancing, he thought, the smile wiped away as fast as it had come.

As though she read his mind she put a hand on his arm and said, "For each thing you cannot do, there are a dozen others you can."

He looked down at her quizzically. "Do you know me so well, then?"

"I want to. And I know something of your fears, I think. Though I would guess you would rather I did not."

"Witch!" he said with some affection and, for her sake, he forced himself to smile again. "You pluck the thoughts right out of my head."

She shook her head but smiled, pleased by the compliment, for she knew he meant it as such. "Where do we go first?" she asked, turning the subject.

"London, I think. Most of my family will be there and they would never forgive me if I did not go to them first," Harry said with a sigh. "Afterward, well, afterward we can go wherever you wish."

She started to shake her head again but stopped and a mischievous gleam lit her eyes, warning him a moment before she spoke. "The continent? The talks, perhaps?" she asked impishly.

He pretended to frown but could not sustain it long. "Wretch!" he told her. "You would take advantage of a poor, sick man?"

"Yes."

He laughed. He could not help himself. There was such joy in being with her that even in the depths of his fears, late at night, it helped to see her lying close beside him. And when she teased, as she did now, there were moments when he felt he could face whatever lay ahead.

"No, we are not going to the continent," he told her firmly. "Not unless I am sent."

"But why not?"

"Because I would be useless there," Harry replied, and there was no mistaking the sincerity behind the words. "Nor could I protect you if something were to go wrong and the French decided to break the treaty."

She opened her mouth to argue, then closed it again. "Very well," she said.

"Very well?" he echoed warily.

She nodded. He studied her for some moments. "Now why do I not believe you?" he asked aloud.

She grinned, unrepentantly. "Because you know me very well?" she suggested.

"No doubt."

"Well, for once I mean it. I shan't plague you, if you truly do not wish to go," she said and this time it was he who did not doubt her sincerity, though he could not fathom why she might have changed her mind.

And then they were docking. The deck became a fury of activity and slowly Prudence and Harry made their way toward the ramp that would let them off the ship. Each step on that ramp jarred Harry's leg, even though he leaned heavily on the cane as the surgeon had told him to do. But he bit back every exclamation of pain. He would not let anyone know how much this simple thing cost him. Not when other men were having to be carried off on litters.

They had scarcely reached solid ground when Harry heard his name called out. He winced and turned to greet his brother George.

"There you are. Had a devil of a time getting the coach close enough. But it's straight over here, Harry. We'll have you home before you know it. And who is this, a camp follower turned nurse? You may send her off for we've engaged the best of care for you."

Harry felt rather than saw the chagrin on Prudence's face. Hastily he spoke to head off what he instinctively knew would be trouble.

"George, if you received my letter that I was returning home—"

But his brother cut him off before he could say anything more. "Letter? No we've received no letter.

Not from you. But Sir Thomas received word, don't ask me how, that you were injured and would be returning home on this ship. So naturally I came to get you. Here, my good woman, here is something for your trouble and I said you may take yourself off. As you can see, my brother is in my charge now."

"George," Harry had to all but yell to get his brother's attention, "this is not a camp follower or a nurse. This is my wife. Prudence, this is my brother, Lord Darton."

"Wife?" George gaped at him. "Surely you are joking? You cannot have married someone like this!"

Now the devil was in it and Harry was not quick enough. Prudence spoke before he had even begun to frame his reply.

"I assure you, Lord Darton, that I am indeed Harry's wife. And before you say anything more, anything you may later regret, let me inform you that my birth is equal to his. My uncle is a diplomat in the king's service and my father was Lord Marland." She paused, then added almost graciously, "I can well understand your confusion, however. My attire is borrowed and not of the quality to which I am accustomed. I must hope it can be replaced quickly, now that we are back in England."

Harry rather enjoyed the sight of his brother's stunned expression. And the way he changed sides the moment he realized what Prudence was saying. When she finally finished her little speech, George even managed a smile, albeit a weak one, and his color was still a little high.

"Er, my profound apologies for the misunderstanding. That is to say, welcome to the family. But, er, Harry? I do think it would be best to continue this discussion in the coach, rather than providing a spectacle for everyone."

Harry offered his arm to Prudence and she took it, very much as though she were a grande dame instead of the woman who had masqueraded as a very dirty gypsy boy such a short time before. George mopped his brow as he led the way to the coach. The moment they were in sight, the footman leapt to open the coach door.

"My man, Wilkins, is bringing our baggage," Harry said. "Someone ought to keep watch for him."

"No need," Prudence said softly. "He has seen us and is coming this way."

With patent relief, George gave orders for the footman to help Wilkins strap the baggage on back and make room for him to ride beside the coachman. And then they were off for London, moving slowly at first but then more quickly as they quit the seaside town.

It was, Harry had to admit, a welcome thought, that he would travel in such a well sprung vehicle. And that his brother had cared enough to come and collect him. Now if he could just prevent George and Prudence from coming to blows on the journey home. That, unfortunately, seemed an impossible task but at least, he consoled himself, he need not fear the journey would be boring.

"Er, how did you and my brother come to meet?" George asked, when their things had been strapped onto the back and the coach was on its way. "Was your uncle at the court of the king of Spain?"

Prudence flushed. Harry grinned at her wickedly and he had the distinct impression that had George not been there she would have stuck her tongue out at him. Of course, if George had not been there, she would have had no reason to do so.

She looked away, careful not to meet Harry's eyes as she replied, "Why no, Lord Darton. Harry and I, er, met when I was, that is to say, what I mean is—"

Harry took pity on her. "What she means to say is that she fell overboard from the ship she was on and she happened to wash ashore just where I was. I rescued her and we, er, became rather, er, attached to one another."

George regarded him with a shrewdness Harry sometimes forgot his eldest brother possessed. "Coming it much too brown, Harry. I know a Banbury tale when I hear one! The truth now."

"The truth?" Prudence asked, leaning forward. "The truth is that I fell overboard, your brother rescued me, we fled through France dressed as a priest and nun, were captured by the French, escaped, then traveled about dressed as two gypsy brothers. Eventually we managed to reach Spain and the Marquess of Wellington's camp where we were married within days of our arrival."

George went very pale and then flushed a deep crimson. His voice shook almost as much as the finger he pointed at her as he said, "Young woman I will not be made game of. If you do not wish to confide in me, simply say so. But do not tell me tales even a child would know enough to disbelieve."

Prudence tilted up her chin and leaned back against the squabs. "Yes, Lord Darton," she said with a meekness Harry knew far better than to trust.

But George did not know her and he merely nodded. "Good. That's settled then. Obviously you do not wish me to pry and I shan't. But I do need to know something of what to tell the *ton* when I am asked about your marriage, Harry."

The colonel rubbed his chin and looked at Prudence. "There is some sense to that," he told her. "If we do not wish to be the cause of foolish speculation, then we must tell them something. What do you wish my brother to say? What should *we* say?"

She thought about it for a long moment, then her smile lit up her face and even George seemed taken aback by how much it altered her appearance.

"We shall say that my uncle wished to take me to the talks on the continent with him but that you and I had met—somewhere—and developed a *tendre* for one another. I could not bear to be parted from you so I went to Spain instead. And we were married. I would have returned to England alone save that you were wounded and needed me so we returned together."

"Yes, but where did the two of you meet?" George demanded of Prudence. "Here in England? I don't recall seeing you at Almack's or any other ball."

Harry waved a careless hand. "Somewhere. We cannot say precisely where because it is a place I am not supposed to have been. A secret mission, you understand. And indeed," he said with a fond look at Prudence, "it is the truth."

She reached out a hand to him. "So it is," she agreed.

George snorted. "Very well. If you want me to tell a Banbury tale, a Banbury tale it shall be. But don't blame me if it ain't believed!"

Chapter 13

If Lord Darton had been skeptical, his wife Athenia was even more so. To be sure, she was polite enough to Prudence in the drawing room as Harry was settled onto a sofa by the fire. His face was white and drawn with pain from the journey and it had taken two footmen to help carry him up the stairs.

"Come, my dear, I shall show you to your room. You will no doubt wish to refresh yourself," Lady Darton said to Prudence.

"Thank you, I should," she agreed.

As they mounted the stairs to the next floor where the bedrooms were all to be found, Prudence said, "I thank you for being so kind to me, Lady Darton. I collect Harry's letter had not yet reached you and so you cannot have been expecting him to bring home a wife."

With each word, Athenia's back had straightened more and more until it seemed ramrod stiff. As was her voice as she replied, "Let us have a clear understanding. You may have cozened my husband with your tale of romance, and I do not dispute that your birth is well enough, but I am not so easily taken in. You will have to show me you are worthy of being Harry's bride before I shall accept you as such."

"I see."

"Do you? Probably not. But you will. The only reason I did not say anything in the drawing room is that I would not distress Harry for the world. Particularly as injured as he is now."

Prudence lifted her eyebrows. "But you will distress him if you cause me any trouble, whether it is today or at a later time."

"Indeed?" Lady Darton asked, with a sour smile. "Perhaps, perhaps not. If he discovers himself to be mistaken in your character, then he may be grateful to me for taking his part."

Now Prudence was confused. She tilted her head to one side as she regarded Lady Darton. After a long moment her expression softened and she almost smiled as she said, "You care about Harry very much, don't you?"

"Of course I do," Lady Darton replied. "It is my duty to do so."

Prudence did smile then. She slipped an arm through Lady Darton's, ignoring that lady's gasp of outrage. "We both care for Harry and I think it is more than duty on your part. Which makes us friends, even though I know it will take you some time to believe it. For now I am simply grateful that you sent a coach for him and are taking him, indeed both of us, into your home. Harry has been subject to the megrims ever since he was injured and it is more than I can do to raise his spirits out of them. For that I think he needs your help. And Lord Darton's."

By the end of this speech Lady Darton no longer looked quite so angry. She did not smile, perhaps, but there was a hint of softness about her eyes and in her voice.

"We shall do what we can. And you are welcome in my house."

It was a beginning. For now, Prudence thought, that was as much as she could hope to have. Moving in diplomatic circles had taught her to take victory where she could and then retreat to plan her strategy for the next encounter. One had to think like one's opponent and in Lady Darton's place Prudence had to admit that she would have been just as suspicious.

When she had taken off her bonnet and cloak and

gloves and brushed the tangles out of her hair, Prudence returned to the drawing room. There she paused in the doorway, watching Harry. His color had started to come back, no doubt aided by the glass of wine in his hand.

But he was also laughing at something Lord Darton was saying to him and for that Prudence could only be grateful. In spite of herself, in spite of the temper both Lord and Lady Darton had roused in her, she smiled. It was then that Harry turned his head and saw her. A look passed between them and her wayward thoughts could only think of the bed above and how soon Harry would be ready to share it.

But his thoughts were on other matters. "Come meet the rest of my scapegrace family," he said, calling her into the room.

It was only then that Prudence realized there were others present. She went to stand by Harry and he pulled her down to sit beside him on the couch, one comforting—if scandalous—arm about her waist.

"This is my brother Philip, the barrister, and his wife, Emily. This is my brother James and his wife, Juliet. And this is Sir Thomas Levenger and Lady Levenger. Everyone, this is my wife, Prudence."

They were all kind. Far kinder than Prudence felt she deserved. And yet she was grateful for Harry's sake for she could see that it put his mind at rest to see them accept her so readily. It was only Prudence who noticed the reserve in their eyes even as they smiled and greeted her.

But again, who was she to say they were wrong? If she thought anyone threatened Harry she would have been far more blunt and challenging than these kind people. It was evident they loved Harry, too.

Again the story was told, such as it was. And again she could see the reservations in their eyes. But they were all polite enough to pretend to believe it. There were more polite words and finally it was Sir Thomas who touched on the matter that worried them all the most.

"How are you, Harry? Truly? And no false courage now. We want to know, what does the surgeon say about your leg?" he asked, coming to rest a hand on Harry's shoulder.

The arm around Prudence's waist tightened. And she could hear the constraint in his voice as he answered. "The surgeons can tell me very little save that my leg was badly injured and we must wait to see how much use of it I will have when all is said and done."

Sir Thomas looked at Prudence and quirked an eyebrow upward. Was that where Harry had learned the trick? She looked at Harry and she looked at Sir Thomas and all she could do was shrug her shoulders and shake her head.

"I know no more than Harry," she told him. "The surgeons could tell us no more."

"But the Marquess of Wellington says Harry is to sell out his commission," Lord Darton protested. "Surely he would not say so unless he knew full well the extent of the injury. You need not cavil to tell us the truth, Harry!"

From the way his eyes widened with dismay, Prudence knew that this was the first Harry had heard any such thing, just as it was the first time for her. He was too stunned to speak and so she did so for him.

In a voice cold as ice she asked, "Where, my lord, did you hear such a calumny? Wellington made no such request of Harry that I heard."

"Er, that is, Sir Thomas you tell them!"

A look of irritation crossed the elder man's face but he rid himself of it quickly. Instead he looked at Harry, careful to meet his eyes squarely.

"I have had word that Wellington does not think you will return to his staff. That he does indeed expect you to sell out your commission. But he is not pleased to think this must be so."

"And how the devil would you know such a thing?" Harry demanded, his voice shaking.

Sir Thomas did not even blink. In a soft voice that was meant to be soothing he said gently, "The same way I knew which ship was bringing you home, though I wish someone had thought to mention your bride! Come, I do not mean to distress you, my boy. I hope, we all hope, that you make a full recovery. And if you do, Wellington will welcome you back with great delight."

But the damage was already done. Prudence could see the strain in Harry's face. "Perhaps," she suggested to the others, "Harry should rest now?"

"Yes, of course," Lord Darton said instantly.

"We have had a room made up on this level," Lady Darton added, "so that he need not deal with stairs."

Prudence would have gone with him, but Harry's brothers all crowded around to help him up and she guessed that he would not thank her for hovering. And when they were gone from the room Sir Thomas smiled at her.

"Wise woman," he said. "Perhaps Harry chose more shrewdly than we guessed."

Prudence wanted to be offended but, as so many had discovered before her, she could not resist that smile. Or the frank and friendly way Lady Levenger slipped an arm around her husband's waist and added, "Welcome to the family, my dear. We are very happy to have you."

Harry didn't want to lean on his brothers but he found he had no choice. The journey had fatigued him more than he expected and had they not been holding him up, he knew he would have fainted.

But because they were his brothers, they knew better than to offer him sympathy. Instead, they roasted him unmercifully, a kindness for which he was profoundly grateful.

"What? You are weak as a kitten," Philip teased.

"Your wife did not look such a termagant to me but she seems to have worn you out entirely."

"No, no, it is all a ploy to get our sympathy!" James countered. "We are to wait on him hand and foot and do his bidding. I have always known it was his dream to order us about."

Even George could not resist. There was, most astonishingly, a twinkle in his eyes as he said, "No, no, I think this is not for our benefit but for that of his wife. Can you not imagine her bending over him, doing whatever he wished, and being most solicitous? Why, I do believe he has hit upon the perfect way to make a wife hold her tongue and show him only tenderness and sweetness."

The sight of their utterly staid brother making such a joke was enough to render both Philip and James speechless. But Harry grinned and retaliated in kind.

"Ah, but George, you would first have to endure the dirt and mud of a battlefield and I do not think you would like it, for it would do horrible things to your clothes."

Lord Darton snorted. "Perhaps. But we could send James. He has nothing to do and we could see if it worked with him before Philip and I risked offending our tailors in such a way."

"Here, no!" James said holding up a hand in mock fright. "I might miss a ball or card party and offend the hostess forever."

"Besides," Philip chimed in, "Harry has already taken this tack and it really is not the thing to imitate a fellow in such a blatant way. We should have to find some unexceptional way that no one would realize what we were about. And how could we be certain our wives would not terrorize us, keeping us helpless, rather than tending to us as sweetly as his wife is? Brilliant as Harry's plan has been, I am not at all sure it would work with Emily."

By this time they had managed to maneuver Harry into the room and help him into the bed. Wilkins stood respectfully to the side, watching the roasting with patent approval in his eyes.

James set the cane close to Harry's hand. "In case you find the need to get up on your own later," he explained.

And then there was nothing more to be done. The pillows had been fluffed twice and the coverlet settled just so. The three men looked at one another with uncertainty. It was Harry's soft voice that put them at ease.

"Thank you," he said. "I am more grateful than you can know to have such wonderful fellows for brothers. No, I shan't embarrass you further except to say that it is good to be home. And I expect to bedevil all of you before I am done."

They laughed, then, at these last words. And with a few more crude jests and abjurations for Harry to rest, they shuffled out of the room, reluctant to leave him alone. They glanced at Wilkins but he only shrugged.

"Go! Leave me!" Harry ordered. "I am tired of seeing the lot of you!"

They went, and Harry knew it was because they could see the fatigue in his face. As he lay back against the pillows he felt the strongest urge to curse his fate, to rail against what could not be changed.

But he did not. Instead, as Wilkins quietly drew the curtains and straightened a few things, Harry pondered his future. To be sure, there was a slight chance he would recover completely. In which case matters were simple. He would be back with Wellington the moment the surgeons pronounced him well enough to do so.

But what if he did not? He could not, would not contemplate a lifetime of idle dissipation.

Even as he tried to wrestle with the problem, Harry slipped into sleep. And that was how Prudence found him, some time later. He never saw her or felt her hand on his brow. He slept too deeply for that. Nor did he hear her ask Wilkins how he did or hear the soft reply that all was as well as might be expected.

Chapter 14

Prudence was just leaving her room to go down to dinner when she heard the noises. Giggling and shushing noises. Feet running in the hallway above. Intrigued, she began to climb up the stairs. Before she reached the next floor she was confronted by four faces that stared at her avidly. There were two boys and two girls, ranging in age, she guessed, from eight to two years old. The baby ought not to have been out of the nursery. But then none of them should have been out of the nursery at this hour of the day.

"Are you Uncle Harry's wife?" the eldest boy asked.

Prudence nodded.

"We want to see him."

She blinked. All four faces regarded her with grim determination. More than one lower lip trembled.

"Is he going to die?"

That was the girl, and impulsively Prudence swept her up into a hug. "No! Of course not!" she said, shocked that the child would think such a thing.

But they all did. She could see it in their faces. Without thinking about it, she sat down on the top step of the stairs so that they could crowd around her.

"Your Uncle Harry is going to be fine," she said. "He's been hurt and the surgeon says it will take time to heal. There may be some things he can never do, but he isn't going to die."

"Is he going to be crippled?"

Prudence took a deep breath. Clearly there was only

one thing to do. Gathering up the youngest child in her arms and holding out her hand to the second youngest she said, "Why don't I take you to see him and you can judge for yourself how serious his condition might be."

The younger kids came readily but the eldest held back. "We're not supposed to bother him," he told her.

Her smile softened even more. "It's all right," she answered gently. "If anyone says you ought not to be there I shall say that I gave you direct orders to come and raise your uncle's spirits, okay?"

"Will it?" the second oldest child, a girl, asked anxiously.

Prudence nodded. "I truly think it will."

She couldn't know that for sure, of course. Perhaps Harry found his nephews and nieces a confounded nuisance. She only knew that they were upset and worried and she was doing the one thing that might reassure them. And that, at the moment, was all that seemed to matter.

Of course, what seemed so simple upstairs became far more complicated when she reached the drawing room and found not only Harry, but Lord and Lady Darton there. At the sight of them, Lady Darton rose to her feet.

"You were supposed to stay upstairs, children. Uncle Harry isn't well."

"Oh, let them come see him," Lord Darton countered carelessly. "I suppose they can do no harm if they spend just a few minutes with him."

Prudence noted that Harry visibly braced himself and even looked a trifle pale as he stared at the children. What on earth was wrong with everyone? Instantly she made a decision. She stopped the children before they could run into the room, as they clearly intended to do.

With a firm but friendly voice she said, "You must all go in quietly. No running. And no clambering upon your Uncle Harry's lap. I shall expect your assistance in seeing to it that he is not discomforted in any way. Can I count on all of you?"

They stared at her, she thought, with such astonishment that it was as though she had suddenly overturned their world. And as if they meant to disobey.

"If you don't," she said, raising her eyebrows and planting one hand on each hip, "it's straight back upstairs you shall go! And not another chance to see your Uncle Harry while we are staying here."

For a long moment, matters hung in the balance. She had never, Prudence thought, faced a more hostile crowd. But then, suddenly the eldest drew in a deep breath, drew himself up straight.

"I promise we shall be careful. And none of you," he told his siblings in a stern voice, "are to cause Uncle Harry the least distress."

They nodded solemnly and then filed into the room slowly, cautiously, and quietly. They went over to Harry and while they surrounded him, they were careful not to actually touch him.

"Are you all right?"

"You're not going to die, are you?"

"Or be crippled?"

Only the youngest couldn't ask any questions but even he stared worriedly at Harry. Suddenly the look on the colonel's face softened. He looked at them each in turn. Then, as solemnly as they had asked him their questions, he answered them.

"I am going to be fine. I am not going to die. I am not going to lose my leg, if that is what you fear. I shall even, soon enough, be able to chase you around the park and catch you," he concluded with a growl that seemed to delight the children.

Prudence dearly hoped that was true. Not only because the children patently wanted it to be, but for Harry's sake as well. For the first time since the battle, a little of the pinched look had left his face and she

was very grateful to see a hint of the smile she loved
so dearly.

A glance showed her that Lord and Lady Darton
were also staring at Harry, but almost as if they had
never seen him before. And they were giving their
offspring even stranger looks.

The children were oblivious. The eldest held out a
hand to his uncle and said, "I'm very glad to hear
it, sir."

Harry took his nephew's hand and then the others
moved closer, too. But this time, instead of wariness
there was a look of calm and indeed almost pleasure
on his face.

From the other side of the room Lord Darton
spoke, his tone jovial. "If she weren't your wife,
Harry, I'd say we should hire her as a governess to
these brats. I've never seen them so well behaved!"

Harry flushed, betraying the fact that neither had
he. The children, on the other hand, began to visibly
bristle at the insult. Particularly when Lady Darton
said thoughtfully, "Perhaps we ought to look into hir-
ing someone like her, George."

Prudence could guess only too well what the suddenly sullen looks on the children's faces portended.
Hastily she intervened.

"Well, I think them marvelously well-behaved children. And expect them to remain so. For I shall need
them to help me coax Harry into the exercise the surgeon recommended. Will you help me?" she asked
the four children.

Four vigorous nods answered her and the sullen
looks vanished as quickly as they had come.

"We should be happy to."

"How can we help?"

"Uncle Harry, you'd like us to help, wouldn't you?"

Uncle Harry looked anything but delighted. Still, he
managed to smile and reply, manfully, "Of course. My
wife will tell you how you can, er, help."

"Good. Now, children, I expect your uncle is tired.

Why don't we go back upstairs and you can show me your portion of the house. I can't stay long for I am needed back downstairs soon but there should be time for a very quick tour."

Whether it was because she had them thoroughly cowed, or because she had purposely not used the word nursery to the children, they agreed without arguing. A circumstance that once again seemed to astonish everyone else in the room. But they very politely took their leave of the adults as though they behaved this way every day.

Then, once again holding the hands of the two youngest, Prudence led the children out of the room and up the stairs. There she found several cozy rooms, all outfitted nicely for children. In the largest room was a table and chairs, bookshelves, and a young man who had the most harassed look on his face that she had ever seen. At the sight of them, he gave a gasp of relief, then began to lecture.

"I told you children not to leave the schoolroom! I only went to my room for a moment and you were to stay here, playing quietly. Not disturbing the adults in the house."

"It was my fault," Prudence said gently. "I gave them permission to come downstairs to see their Uncle Harry."

The man threw up his hands. "You gave your permission. And did it never occur to you to consult with me, first? Of course not! Nor with Nurse, I suppose. She has been frantic looking for the littlest ones. They were to have had their baths now. The schedule for the day is in tatters. Who the devil are you, anyway?"

She felt a trifle abashed and almost apologized. But the children were looking at her with such pleas in their eyes that, instead, she stood her ground.

"I am Mrs. Langford. Colonel Langford's wife. And I am very sorry if I disrupted the schedule, but it was important," Prudence said coolly.

He gaped at her and she pressed her advantage. "I

believe there may be more times this week that I shall need to take the children downstairs. I shall try to alert you ahead of time, but that may not always be possible."

"Take them downstairs?" the tutor echoed. "Why on earth should you wish to do that? Lord and Lady Darton always come up here when they wish to see their children."

"But Colonel Langford cannot climb the stairs as yet," Prudence said gently. "The children must come to him."

The tutor looked at her as if she had lost her wits and Prudence began to think that perhaps she had. Nor did it help that when he spoke, the tutor's voice was tart and sarcastic.

"Oh, and I suppose the colonel has asked for them? Naturally he did so. Nevermind that the entire staff knows that Lord Darton's brothers greatly dis—"

Prudence cut him off before he could complete the words. In a bright, cheerful, and very loud voice she said, "Lord Darton's brothers greatly dislike to be a nuisance! But Colonel Langford was injured in Spain and asked the children to help him get the exercise the surgeon recommended in order for his leg to heal properly."

The tutor looked as if he would like to call her a liar to her face but did not quite dare. So he swallowed hard, bowed, and said, with a resigned sigh, "Of course, Mrs. Langford. But do, I pray, give me warning next time?"

"Of course, sir," she answered in almost precisely the same tone as he.

The man seemed to relax then and turned to the children. He spoke a trifle sharply, telling the little ones to go in to the nursery where Nurse was waiting for them, and he told the older two to go and find books to read.

When they would have objected, wanting to spend more time with Prudence, she said, quite firmly, "No.

I shall see you another day. For now you are to listen to your tutor."

He looked surprised but pleased by her support, as if it were something to which he was unaccustomed. Indeed his voice thawed perceptibly.

If they did not part precisely as friends, at least they parted on amicable terms. Downstairs, outside the drawing room, Prudence found Lady Darton waiting for her and she did not look pleased at all.

"Are my children back in the schoolroom?" she asked stiffly.

"Yes. The two youngest are about to take a bath, the two eldest are with their tutor."

Prudence eyed Lady Darton warily. Abruptly Athenia seemed to come to some decision for she said, "Come, let us go to my private parlor. I know that dinner is waiting but I should like to speak with you alone first."

To ring a peal over her head no doubt, Prudence thought as she followed Lady Darton to a room at the back of the house. There Athenia turned to face Prudence. Her voice was severe but there was a betraying quiver as she said, "How did you know how to do that?"

Prudence blinked. "Know how to do what?"

"Speak to my children as you did. Bring them to see Harry. I shouldn't have dared. He thinks I don't know but he doesn't like my children. At least I should have said so before today. None of my husband's brothers like my children. And there are moments when I cannot blame them," she said, the quiver more pronounced now.

Prudence could not think of a single word to answer and so she simply waited. After a moment Lady Darton began to pace about the room, her hands clasped in front of her.

"I try to be an excellent mother. I am just like my own. And yet it does not seem to be enough. Nor does George, Lord Darton know how to handle matters any better than I. I thought we were doing well. I thought my husband's brothers merely prejudiced against children. But today, when I saw how my children could behave, when I saw how Harry looked at them when they did, then I knew that I was mistaken. So I ask you again, how did you know what to do?"

Prudence felt a strong impulse to flee the room. Instead she sank onto the sofa. "I suppose," she said slowly, "it is that I can still remember so clearly how it felt to be a child. What I wanted and what I needed."

Lady Darton came to sit on the sofa beside Prudence. Her brow was wrinkled as she said, "I had not thought to try to remember. I thought it enough to simply do as my parents had done."

"I am the niece of a diplomat, and my father was a diplomat as well," Prudence said with a wry smile. "I have heard from my earliest days that one must endeavor to think as the other person thinks, to feel as the other person feels. It would seem to apply as much to children as to foreigners."

"Or," Athenia said, an odd and faraway look in her eyes, "perhaps husbands as well?"

Prudence blinked in some surprise. "Why, yes," she said slowly. "Husbands as well."

They looked at one another and then Athenia and Prudence both started to giggle. And that was the odd sight that greeted Lord Darton when he came in search of his wife and guest.

Chapter 15

The first week was something of a trial for everyone. Harry's homecoming was not what anyone, including Harry, had ever expected. And Prudence was a decided complication. She turned Lord Darton's household upside down without even seeming to mean to do so and the Langfords were hard put to comprehend her.

It was not that she tried to cause trouble. It was simply that she did not seem to understand the nature of the way things were done in Lord Darton's household. She thought nothing of descending to the kitchen herself to fix Harry a particular food she thought he would like rather than conveying her orders to the staff.

To be sure, she did so in such a way that she did not offend the cook. And indeed she fast became a favorite among the staff. But it was, nonetheless, most disconcerting to Lord and Lady Darton, who were not accustomed to any guest taking such liberties in their household.

Nor did she refrain from giving her opinion upon a great many subjects that Lord Darton had always considered to be beyond the sphere of a lady. It was not, precisely, that he disagreed with her so much that he was simply stunned to have her render any opinion at all.

And Lady Darton was hard put to know what to think as she watched Prudence with the children and with Harry. Had she but known it, the emotion so strong in her breast resembled nothing so much as envy. And it was a sensation she had never felt before.

So it was that a week after her arrival George and Athenia met in Lord Darton's study to discuss their new sister. And their discomfort over her presence in their household.

"What do you think of Harry's wife?" Lord Darton asked cautiously. "She seems most unconventional to me."

"She means well. And she is very fond of Harry, I think. She seems also, I think, capable of being a perfect lady when she decides to do so," Lady Darton replied, choosing her words carefully. "And with some of my dresses made over for her, she looks the part."

He was not convinced. "I know that she has been raised in diplomatic circles and one ought to find that encouraging but there are times when she says the most appalling things," Lord Darton said with pardonable exasperation. "You know everyone will be watching and wondering about her. There are the most outrageous rumors about how she and Harry met and how they came to be married. What will she say or do if someone says such things to her directly?"

With the air of one taking a necessary but unpalatable medicine, Athenia replied, "We shall have to give a small party in their honor. If it is seen that we give Harry and Prudence our support no one will dare cavil at their marriage. London is rather thin of company at the moment but all the better. They will not be faced with a crush of people."

"You do not mind?" George asked his wife doubtfully.

Athenia realized, with some surprise, that she did not mind at all. Perhaps Prudence had influenced her more than she knew, for suddenly she found herself behaving in the oddest manner. She and George had been sitting on sofas that faced one another but now she moved to sit at his side. She also took his hand in hers, startling both of them. It was an oddly pleasant gesture.

"Harry is your brother," she said. "For that reason alone I should do everything in my power to help him."

George blinked at her, then dared to slip his other arm around her waist. Cheered by the fact that she did not draw away, he even dropped a kiss on her forehead.

"You do not dislike having to appear to approve of Prudence?" he asked with some concern.

Lady Darton avoided her husband's eyes. "I, er, Prudence is not perhaps what I would have chosen for Harry, but I think she will suit him."

"You do?" Lord Darton peered closely at his wife. "Are you feeling well, my dear?"

Athenia looked at him then and a tiny corner of her mouth turned up into a smile. There was an oddly shy look on her face that reminded him of when they were courting, as she said, "She loves him, George. Truly loves him."

"But when have you ever cared for that?" he asked, taken aback. "I cannot recall the number of times you have called love a vulgar emotion!"

If he expected her to look away, he was once again mistaken. She held his eyes with her own and her voice was remarkably steady as she said, "I used to think so. But I have begun to think, perhaps, that I have been mistaken. You and I, we were married for sensible reasons. Your father's estate marched with that of my father. We were both sensible people, not given to vulgar displays of emotion. We both held rigid views of what was right and proper."

"And that's just as it should be," he said stoutly.

"Perhaps," she allowed. "But perhaps there is, or could be, something more."

Now a look of alarm crossed Lord Darton's face and he pulled both his arm from around her waist and his hand out of hers.

"What are you trying to say?" he asked, a hint of alarm patent in his voice. "Are you . . . are you trying to say that you have developed a *tendre* for someone?"

Now it was Lady Darton who looked a little afraid. But she swallowed hard and gathered up her courage. "Yes," she said.

He rose to his feet and began to pace about the room. "Who?" he asked at last.

She gaped at him. "Why, George, I am talking about you!"

"Me?" He looked utterly taken aback. "You are talking about me?"

Lady Darton blushed and nodded. Lord Darton came a little closer. He peered closely at her face.

"You don't wish to have an affair with someone else?" he asked, his voice still full of doubt.

Now she looked up at him, not hiding anything as she said, her voice husky with unaccustomed emotion, "Oh, George! I only want to have an affair with *you*!"

And that was why, half an hour later, the major domo stormed into the kitchens vowing to give notice immediately. For, as he said, "I chose to work here precisely because I knew it would be such a properly run house. But if the master and mistress are going to take to such goings on right in the master's study, well, it is more than a body should be expected to bear!"

That, naturally, led to the other servants crowding around and demanding to know what he meant by "goings on." The major domo felt a little relief in being able to describe in great detail the scandalous scene he had walked in upon. Tomorrow he would be overcome with shame at having been so indiscreet as to share this scene with anyone other than the house-keeper, but for the moment, he could not resist telling his tale.

Fortunately for Lord and Lady Darton, most of their servants were secret romantics and, for the first time since coming to this house, began to think of the master and mistress with genuine affection.

It was a presumption that would have offended Lord and Lady Darton. Nonetheless, it did lead to an immediate improvement in the level of happiness among the staff and the quickness with which they moved to serve.

Still, the interruption was enough to recall Lord and Lady Darton to their circumstances. As soon as was practical they did up each other's clothes and made the mutual decision to go upstairs. That was how Harry came to meet them in the hallway.

"George?" Harry said, trying very hard to pretend he did not see that his brother's buttons had been done up wrong.

"Er, yes, Harry? Is it urgent?"

"No, no, not urgent at all," the colonel hastily replied. "I shall talk with you later. Er, your servant, Lady Darton."

She blushed most becomingly and for the first time Harry began to understand what had drawn his brother to this woman. It was an entirely new vision for Harry and it was all he could do to bow and back away from the pair and reach the library before he collapsed in laughter on the so recently vacated sofa.

That was where Prudence found *him*.

"Are you all right?" Prudence asked doubtfully from where she stood in the doorway.

Harry waved to her. "Come in. And for heaven's sake close that door! If any of the servants should see us we would be done for."

Warily Prudence did as she was bid. She came to stand over Harry and feel his forehead with her hand. "Are you certain you are all right?" she asked again.

Harry choked back another snort of laughter. "Absolutely," he told her solemnly.

Now her eyes narrowed. "Then what," she asked, tapping her foot impatiently, "is this all about?"

Harry reached up a hand and drew her down to his

side. Or at least that was what he thought he intended. Instead, somehow she ended up sitting on his lap. Which was not, he thought, an altogether bad thing.

It only took a moment for him to undo the strings of her bonnet. Another moment to pull off the gloves she still wore and toss them aside.

"Harry?" she asked uncertainly. "What are you doing?"

"Repeating, I think, what my oh-so-proper brother and his wife just did in this room."

Prudence blinked at him. "Lord and Lady Darton?"

Harry solemnly nodded and Prudence first stared, then began to giggle. "Just what I thought," he told her teasingly.

She reached up to wind her arms around his neck. "And where should we start?" she asked.

In answer, he bent his head to kiss her. And for the first time since the battle he let his hands touch her, really touch her.

She pulled back. "Harry?" she asked uncertainly.

"Yes?"

"Are you well enough for this?"

He kissed the tip of her nose and grinned. "I think so. And more importantly, so does the rest of me. But perhaps not in here, after all."

In an instant she was off his lap and on her feet. As she gave him a hand to help him up she saw him wince. "I hurt you!" she said in dismay.

He winced again. "Perhaps a little," he allowed. "I ought not to have had you sit on my lap quite yet, I think. But," he told her, kissing the hand holding his, "do not think that means I mean to let you escape, madam."

"No?" a half-hesitant, half-teasing note crept into her own voice. "What do you mean to do with me?"

His eyes were warm on hers and his voice was husky as he said, "Perhaps we should go to my room and I can simply show you."

"Perhaps."

They were smiling foolishly at one another as they slipped down the hallway to the colonel's room. There they found Wilkins straightening Harry's things, but he took one look at the pair, grinned impertinently, and said, "I can see you won't be needing me for a bit, sir."

Then they were alone together. And if it was not perfect, nonetheless it was a promise of what the future might hold as Harry healed even further.

Chapter 16

Prudence couldn't have said exactly when the notion came to her. Maybe it was overhearing Harry talking quietly with Lord Darton about their father. Maybe it was seeing the shadows in his eyes as he stared at a painting of the man. But at some point she knew she wanted to do something to help him and she thought she knew perhaps what to do.

She couldn't help remembering the letter that Harry had mentioned that day in France. The one that had so angered Monsieur Gilbert. Ever since then, she had been wondering who it might have been meant for and she thought perhaps she knew. But she had no proof, nothing beyond her suspicions. There it might have stayed had she not seen the notice in the paper. The very man she suspected was writing his memoirs and wished for an assistant to help him. Why not, Prudence asked herself, apply for the position?

She could claim that she and Harry needed money. It was no doubt true and it would give her the chance to find out more about the man and maybe even proof that he was the traitor she suspected he might be.

Prudence did not tell Harry, of course, what she intended. He had too much pride to like the notion of his wife solving his dilemmas. Too much pride to wish to think she could protect him, instead of the other way around.

So she simply acted.

* * *

Harry stared at his bride. And she glared back at him. "Why should I not?" she demanded.

"Because you are my wife and it is for me to support you, not the other way around!" he thundered. "I will not have my wife become some sort of servant. And especially not to Lord Brandon."

"Oh for heaven's sake!" Prudence exclaimed in exasperation. "I would not be a servant. I told you: Lord Brandon merely needs someone to help catalog his library and sort out his papers. Since he knows my uncle well and knows that I have been in many of the same places he has been posted, Lord Brandon thought I might be able to be of some assistance in writing his memoirs. But if you do not wish me to do so, then of course I shall not."

This last was spoken with such a meek voice that it startled a surprised laugh out of Harry. "Of course?" he echoed, raising his eyebrows endearingly.

"Well," she amended, "of course I shall not, given how agitated the thought makes you and how the surgeons have told me it is important not to let you get upset."

Harry's chin tilted up and he turned his back to her. His posture was stiff and the hands clenched behind him turned almost white, so tight was their grip.

Over his shoulder he said, "It always comes back to that, does it not? My injury. Even a decision such as this is made not with respect to my wishes but because you dare not upset the invalid."

She ran to him then and he could hear her soft footsteps behind him. Still he flinched when she put her hands on his shoulders and rested her head against his back. But she did not let go, she only gripped tighter.

"If you think that," she said into his coat, "then you are an idiot! A lovable idiot but an idiot nonetheless."

Now he turned to look at her and what he saw in her face almost undid him. But he swallowed hard and persisted.

"Am I? You have such a high opinion of me, it seems, madam."

"No. Not at the moment," she said with a shake of her head. "Indeed, I find it hard to reconcile this side of you with the quick-witted fellow who saved us so often with his hastily crafted tales in France."

He wanted so badly to unclasp his hands and hold her. But he could not. "I see no reason for levity," he said, hearing the petulance in his voice and unable to prevent it.

She slipped an arm through his elbow and looked up at him affectionately. "Of course not," she said. "Ever since you were wounded you have been unable to see a reason for levity anywhere. You are wrong, of course. But your feelings are entirely understandable."

"They are, are they?" he growled down at her. "And what else, pray tell, is understandable?"

But she did not quail before his anger. Instead she met his eyes squarely, her voice steady as she said, "It is understandable that you think yourself less a man even though all the rest of us know you are not. It is understandable that you should wallow in self-pity but I think, perhaps, it is time for that to be at an end."

"Self-pity?"

She nodded, her expression tranquil. He wanted to shout at her, to rail at her words, but his voice trailed off before he even began. Because he could not, however much he wished, deny the truth of what she was saying.

"And if," he said, his voice stiff with hurt, "you were right, what then do you suggest? How ought I to perceive my injury?"

She stood on tiptoe and kissed his cheek, surprising him yet again. "I do so love you," she sighed.

"Because I shout at you?" he asked, his forehead creased in a quizzical frown.

She shook her head but did not answer him. Instead she said, tugging him to a seat at the window. "I think you ought to ask at the War Office or perhaps the

Horse Guards if they have work for you. Even if it is but for a short while, surely you could be of use? There must be dispatches to be read or messages intercepted or decisions to be made that might be helped by what we saw and learned in France."

She paused then added, "I have written my uncle. And received a reply. Our news came too late and the damage is already done. He does not say so, but I think England shall regret the treaty that was made. You will be needed when that time comes. Perhaps more than if you were at Wellington's side on the battlefield."

He pressed his lips together in a thin, angry line. But there was a tiny corner of his heart where he hugged her words close to him, and knew she might be right.

First one corner of his mouth quirked up, and then the other, and then he felt himself smile. He raised both her hands to his lips and kissed them. "Confess," he said. "You threatened to work for Lord Brandon only to confound me and bring me to this point!"

She smiled in return but shook her head. "No," she said in the same tranquil voice as before. "I intend to help Lord Brandon. Because he needs my help and I can give it. Besides," she added, a mischievous twinkle in her eyes, "I have heard all my life tales about some of his wilder exploits and I should very much like to know if they were true. And how better to learn than to read a man's memoirs?"

At this Harry's eyes widened and he could not help but object. "You tell me this and think that it will improve my temper? Soften my attitude toward the man? You think that it will make me more eager to allow you into his house, into his company? What if he should offer you some insult?"

Again she shook her head, still smiling, completely unabashed. "Oh, no. Lord Brandon's tastes run to women of a different sort, I assure you."

Harry gritted his teeth. "There are other reasons," he said, "that make it ineligible for you to be there."

"What other reasons?"

"I cannot tell you."

Prudence looked at him, tilted up her chin, and said, "Whatever your reasons, if you will not tell them to me then you cannot expect me to be bound by them. I am going to help Lord Brandon, with or without your permission."

He wanted to argue. He wanted to shake her. He wanted to remind her that she had said, but moments before, that she would abide by his command, that she did not wish to upset him. But he would not plead the cause of his injury, he simply could not do so.

Harry had, moreover, a strong notion it would be of little use and he had been a military man long enough to know that there were times when it was wiser to retreat, to regroup one's forces for a later attempt, than to throw oneself into certain defeat. So now he merely settled for saying, in a mild voice, "Very well. But at the first instance that proves you wrong you are to leave, is that understood?"

"Yes, Harry."

He trusted her meekness no more than she trusted his. Which was wise on both their parts. It was sometimes, he thought, a difficult thing to be married to a woman raised in diplomatic circles and who had, he suspected, learned every trick there was to know about negotiations and even, perhaps, invented a few of her own.

Prudence had not lied to Harry when she told him why she wished to go to work for Lord Brandon. But neither had she told him the entire truth. So it was with a twinge of guilt that she prepared to go to his house later that afternoon. Still, if she were right, in the end Harry would thank her. She hoped.

It was bad enough that she was undertaking this project. Prudence had no wish to flout convention any more than was absolutely necessary, so she took her maid with her. Or to be more precise, one of Lady Darton's maids. She had no doubt the woman would act something in the nature of a spy for her mistress but as Prudence had no intention of doing anything that could be construed as improper, she did not care.

Lord Brandon lived in a neat little town house not far from Lord Darton and his servants were expecting her. The maid was directed belowstairs and Prudence was shown at once into his lordship's study.

"Prudence, how are you!" he said, coming forward to greet her with a jovial grin. "I hope you will not begrudge me the familiarity. I have, after all, known you since you were but a girl."

It was impossible to resist his good humor. Prudence smiled in reply. "I am in excellent health and how about you, sir? When last I saw you, in South America, you were starting to feel the first signs of gout."

He waved away her concern. "Nonsense! I am perfectly fine. And if I feel a twinge or two, upon occasion, it is no more than one would expect. I eat and drink as I please and shall continue to do so up until the day of my death. But you, my dear! I should say that marriage pleases you. I used to worry about you, you know. There was always just a hint of loneliness about your eyes and I do not see it there today."

Her eyes twinkled. "It took me some time to find a man to suit me, but Colonel Langford does so nicely," she agreed in her most demure voice.

Brandon gave a shout of laughter, then waved her to a seat. "I don't know why you should be willing to bother with an old man like myself when you have such a handsome one at home, but I am grateful for your help."

For all the lightness in his voice, there was a question in his lordship's words. A question that must be answered if she were to avoid suspicion.

She met his eyes squarely and spoke what truth she could. "When I was very little, I remember Papa speaking of you with the greatest affection. And Mama saying there was no man, save Papa, who could hold a candle to your talents. When I heard you needed assistance with your memoirs, well, I could not resist the chance to discover if the rumors I have heard all my life are true."

He gave another shout of laughter. His jovial humor was one of the things Prudence had always liked best about the man and she felt a pang of guilt at how she meant to traduce him. But she dared not think about that now. All her focus must be on him.

Lord Brandon wagged an admonitory finger in her direction. "You ought not to admit to such things!" he told her with a twinkle in his eyes that belied the sternness of his voice.

She opened her eyes wide, her hands folded demurely in her lap. "I should never dream of telling anyone but you," she said.

"Mmmm. Well, we had best get started. I cannot think your young husband will be willing to lend you to me often. So the more we can do today the better."

"I agree. Where should you like me to start?" Prudence asked, leaning forward.

Moments later they were deep in discussion and within the hour she was taking notes as he talked in grave tones about matters few women, or even men, were ever privileged to know about. And the more she heard, the more certain Prudence felt that she was right.

It was a very good thing, she thought, that she had taken this post. What she meant to do no one else could have accomplished. As for the consequences, well she would simply not think about those until she had what she wanted in hand. Then and only then would it matter.

Meanwhile, she had best do what Lord Brandon thought she should. And in truth it was no hardship to transcribe the words of a man who by his own account had lead such a fascinating life.

Chapter 17

The small party Lord and Lady Darton planned to hold to introduce Harry and his wife to the *ton* was the subject of a great deal of conjecture. There were those who called upon Lady Darton hoping to catch a glimpse of the couple beforehand.

They were all disappointed. Prudence went to Lord Brandon's town house every day to help him with his memoirs and Harry had taken her advice and was now working at the Horse Guards. He held himself stiffly at first, expecting to find a desk job sadly depressing.

But it wasn't. Instead he found he enjoyed the daily discussions over the meaning of intercepted messages or speculation on what Bonaparte meant to do next. To be sure, he found the situation with the former colonies most distressing but even there his opinions were solicited with gratifying frequency. And Harry began to feel that perhaps he was not so useless after all.

And at night he had Prudence to share his bed. Though his leg still pained him and he could not have sat on a horse, there were other things he could do. Particularly when Prudence showed her inventiveness. And when she sometimes called him "Alain," as if they were still in France, he almost felt happy again.

Indeed, Harry had nearly been lulled into a sense of complacency when the first hint of trouble crossed his desk. It was a copy of a report dated from almost a year before and dealt with the escape of prisoners from Dover Castle. Immediately Harry realized the danger in that. For Dover Castle was where James had arranged to send his signals from. The signals that Phillipe Thierry and Bertrand Vallois in France were collecting and sending on to Wellington. If escaped prisoners took word back to France of what was going on there, the entire project might well be in danger.

"But that was more than a year ago," Sir Thomas pointed out when Harry brought it to his attention as they sat quietly in a corner of White's. "If there were going to be trouble as a result of it, surely it would have already occurred?"

"There is reason to believe the men were recaptured and only recently escaped again," Harry said. "Sir, you helped us plan these signals. What damage do you think such news could produce should word of them reach France?"

The elder barrister was silent for several moments then he sighed. "Unless they could break the code or catch our men receiving them, very little I should think."

Harry nodded. "That does make sense," he admitted. "It is the whole reason we set things up as we did."

"Still, you would wish to warn our man in France?" Sir Thomas suggested shrewdly. When Harry nodded again he said, "Well, that is easy enough to arrange. Let us have Philip's wife put the information in the next article she writes for the paper. Your man will have it within the week."

"That also makes sense," Harry agreed grudgingly.

Sir Thomas regarded the younger man shrewdly. "There is something else bothering you, isn't there?" he asked.

Harry hesitated, then grinned wryly. "No wonder you are so successful in court," he retorted. "A man can hide nothing from you."

"I should hope not," Sir Thomas said with patent surprise. "It is my job to discern the truth. But you will not divert my attention with flattery. What is troubling you?"

"Do you know Lord Brandon?" Harry asked.

It was the barrister's turn to hesitate. "Y-yes."

Harry raised his eyebrows at the curtness of the other man's tone. "Something to his discredit?"

Again the hesitation. "Nothing certain. Perhaps I should ask why you wish to know."

"My wife is working for him."

Now Sir Thomas sat abruptly upright. "What?"

There was unmistakable alarm in his voice. And that only added to Harry's unease.

"Apparently Lord Brandon is writing his memoirs and my wife is assisting him."

"How much does she know of our family affairs? Of our signal system? And what did she see when the two of you were in France?" Sir Thomas demanded.

"The signal system is not mentioned in George's house, since he knows nothing of it. She met one of the men, Bertrand Vallois, when we were in France, but she saw nothing of the system there, either. Still, she saw most of what I saw while we were in France and I cannot guess what she saw in Wellington's camp," Harry answered slowly. "She is the niece of a diplomat and has trained herself to notice whatever she can. Why? Tell me plainly, Sir Thomas, what do you suspect?"

But the other man only shook his head. "I cannot. I must speak to a few people first. Just tell your wife to be careful, will you? Ask her not to speak to him of your adventures."

Harry nodded. He had a great many questions but Sir Thomas was too shrewd a man to berate for holding his counsel. The habit of trust was strong and Harry listened to it now. He rose to his feet as Sir Thomas did and held out his hand.

"Thank you, sir."

"Don't thank me yet, my boy. You may end up

cursing me for what I may have to tell you. But mind
you warn your wife. And Harry?"

"Yes, sir?"

"You might, perhaps, wish to guard your own
tongue with her. Say nothing of what you see or hear
at the Horse Guards, no matter how harmless it
might seem."

Harry nodded, and walked away, out of the club,
with a strong sense of foreboding.

Prudence had no notion of what was taking place
between Harry and Sir Thomas. Instead all her attention was focused on Lord Brandon, who was speaking
with sweeping gestures of his days posted to the court
of Leopold the Second in Austria. And of the lovely
lady with whom he carried on a liaison at the time.

"Beautiful, absolutely beautiful," Lord Brandon
said, a reminiscent smile on his lips. "And totally indiscreet. The things I learned from that woman! A
pity she was later tried for treason by her own coun-
trymen. Such a waste of beauty. But what can one
do?"

He looked at Prudence expectantly and she murmured, "Nothing, I should guess."

"Absolutely right!" he beamed at her. "Write down
that I said one of the greatest lessons I learned was
never to trust a woman with a secret. Impossible to
hold their tongues, you know."

"Indeed?" Prudence countered, a hint of frost in
her voice.

He stared at her blankly, then chuckled. "Don't
mean you, m'dear. You're not a typical woman. Recollect that I've seen you move about in diplomatic circles. Would've made a far better diplomat than your
uncle, I'll tell you that much. And a far prettier one."

Prudence laughed then, her anger forgotten. How
could one hold onto one's temper with a man who
made one laugh in such a way? "If I would, sir, it

is because I watched and learned from men such as yourself," she said.

He wagged a finger at her. "Spanish coin? Fie on you! But I must say, I do hope there is some truth to it. I should like to think so."

"Oh, there is," Prudence said earnestly. "I used to watch you speak to men in a room, knowing just what to say to each one to make them feel your friend. I am afraid I eavesdropped shamelessly."

"Yes, well, it is a talent that takes years to polish," Lord Brandon told her self-consciously. "Mind, you have an innate talent of that sort yourself, I should say. Perhaps we should devote a part of my memoirs to advice I should give to young diplomats aspiring to their first major post?"

"An excellent notion!" Prudence told him approvingly.

"Good. Good. I must think just what I want to say."

"Would you like me to go through old correspondence, while you are thinking, and see if anything looks suitable for inclusion?" Prudence asked.

"No!"

The word was a snarl and Lord Brandon seemed to realize almost instantly just how odd he must sound. Prudence could see him fight for composure. Finally he managed to smooth back his hair as he took a deep breath and say, "That is very kind of you to offer, my child, but it will not be necessary. I shall go through my correspondence myself."

"Oh, good!" Prudence exclaimed with what she hoped was convincing naiveté. "I do so dislike going through men's correspondence. My uncle's is always so deadly boring. Oh, but I didn't mean to offend you! Yours, of course, would be much more interesting, I suppose."

She allowed her voice to trail off so that this last sentence was said with an air of disbelief. Even as she spoke, Prudence could see Lord Brandon relax.

In a far milder voice than before he said, with a

chuckle, "Well, of course, a lady, even such an exceptional lady as yourself, would no doubt think so. Best to leave it to men like myself and your uncle. As boring as it is, we know how to deal with it. Now come and pour me out a cup of this excellent tea my housekeeper has brought us."

Prudence smiled and did so and all the while her mind was busy plotting how she would get her hands on those letters.

Capitaine Jean Louis Dumont stared at the two men standing before him. "Are you certain?" he demanded.

"And as we were leaving the tunnels beneath the castle, we could see, up on the cliff, the light shining out to sea," the first man said.

"Perhaps it is, as our agents have informed us, merely an attempt to lure smugglers to a spot where they can be easily taken," Dumont objected.

The second man shook his head. "I overheard them talking myself, when I was being held outside the governor's office," he said. "It was a means to signal to someone here in France."

"But that makes no sense," the Capitaine countered. "Any signal seen by a British agent could be seen by our people as well."

"But would it mean anything to us?" another man in the room asked quietly. "There have been reports of a light shining from a distance. But it was assumed the light came from a ship and we did not think it important."

Capitaine Dumont considered the situation for several moments. Finally he shook his head. "It still makes no sense to me. But I shall send you on to Paris. And perhaps, just perhaps, it would explain the presence of an English colonel in our midst. Very well, be ready to leave for Paris in the morning."

When the two men were gone, the other man looked at Dumont. "Do you believe them, sir?"

Capitaine Dumont looked at his aide-de-camp. "I

don't know," he said. "Perhaps they will be able to sort out the matter in Paris. But I do not see what good it will do if they cannot tell us how the signals are to be read. Still, perhaps it would be as well if our men on patrol kept their eyes wide for Englishmen traveling from the coast south to Wellington's lines. Or for someone who does not belong where they are. If these men are right, we ought to look for whomever is receiving the signals on this side."

There was a moment's pause as both men recalled the English colonel and the nun who had so briefly been their prisoners. And the account given of their escape by the men who were supposed to escort them back to Paris.

"I shall tell our patrols."

"Yes. Tell them. And if we do capture an English spy, then this time there must be no mistakes, no escapes."

Chapter 18

The *ton* was pleased to be kind. Perhaps it was because they had known Harry for years and he was accounted a war hero who could give them the latest news from Spain. Perhaps it was because Athenia took care to dress Prudence demurely in a new gown of white satin with a ribbon threaded through her hair, a style that made her look younger than her years and far more innocent than anyone seemed likely to otherwise believe.

For as Athenia said the night of the party, "In general I do not like military cant, however I believe that for once it applies. We must marshal our forces but attempt to appear to be weaker than we are so that the enemy does not wage a full-scale attack."

"Are these people the enemy?" Prudence asked doubtfully. "I thought they were your friends."

Athenia paused, as if surprised at the question. "These people are the ones you must win over if you are to be accepted in society. And accepted you must be if Harry is to have the opportunities for advancement that he deserves. Remember who I told you to defer to, which ones to make laugh, and with whom you should say nothing at all and simply cling to Harry's arm lovingly."

Prudence gave a shaky laugh. "And I thought myself to be the diplomat in the house. I had no notion you gave matters such thorough consideration."

Athenia looked at Prudence then dismissed the

maid from the room. When they were alone she drew her to a seat on the chaise longue.

"My dear," Athenia said in a voice more gentle than any Prudence had heard her use thus far, "I understand the *ton*. If I choose to abide by its dictates it is because I understand the consequences so well for those who do not, rather than because I am so enamored of these precepts by nature. I do wish you well. You have brought more joy to Harry these past weeks than I have ever seen in him before. For that my husband and I shall always be very, very grateful. You have also given me much to think about with George. I know you think him a pompous fool and me little better, but I sincerely hope that, in time, we shall come to be friends."

Prudence placed her hand over Lady Darton's. "I should be a poor fool indeed if I did not appreciate what you have done for me. I, too, hope we shall be friends. And I hope you will see that I am not the impulsive fool I sometimes think you believe me to be."

They smiled at each other and then, as though the sentimentality were more than she could bear, Athenia rose to her feet and said briskly, "Come along! They will be gathering downstairs by now and we must be there to greet our guests. Remember, not a word about your time in France!"

In answer, Prudence only gave a mock shudder and followed Lady Darton. Harry, Lord Darton, Philip, James, Sir Thomas, and the other wives were gathered in the drawing room. Small card tables had been set around the room and stood waiting. Servants applied the finishing touches to the arrangement and then discreetly disappeared.

But it was Harry who mattered. At the sight of him, both Athenia and Prudence froze. None of the others in the room looked entirely happy either. "You are wearing your Hussar's uniform," Prudence said unnecessarily.

His voice, when it came, held a biting edge to it. "So I am. As I have already informed my other concerned family members, I am still a soldier. I have not yet sold out my commission."

Prudence stared at him. She felt her heart sink. Surely, she had told herself, he was coming to terms with no longer being a soldier. Now, looking at him, she knew she had been deceiving herself. Harry would never be resigned to being a civilian. Beside her she heard Athenia speak.

"But surely you mean to do so, to sell out shortly?"

Harry glared at Athenia. "Perhaps. But until that day, I am a soldier."

Then he turned his angry, defensive eyes on Prudence, daring her to argue. Instead, she moved to his side and looked up at him, touching his sleeve gently as she did so.

"You look very handsome in your uniform, Harry. And I've no doubt all the women shall be looking daggers at me because you are no longer free to pursue them." Her voice held a teasing note and a smile began to quirk at the corner's of his mouth, almost in spite of himself, she thought. So she pressed on. "You don't want anyone to look at you with pity, do you, Harry. You want them to see the man you have always been."

He nodded, but she could see what the gesture cost him. She squeezed his arm once more then turned to Athenia and said, "Well, how soon do our guests arrive?"

Lady Darton took a deep breath and replied, "Why, right now I suppose."

Then she gave the signal for Lord Darton to open the drawing room doors. Almost immediately the first of the guests was shown in to be announced. And from that moment on, Prudence had not a moment to herself all evening.

Everyone wanted to talk to her. And to Harry who stood at her side, his arm resting lightly on her waist.

Athenia frowned every time she saw it, but Harry only mocked her with his eyes and by the end of the evening Prudence noticed that Lord Darton's arm rested on his wife's waist as well.

Lord Brandon was among the last to arrive and at the sight of him Lord Darton stiffened. Prudence saw him go over and it was clear the meeting was not amicable, though she could not overhear the words.

"What the devil is he doing here?" Harry whispered under his breath beside her. "I cannot believe Lady Darton would have been so foolish as to send him an invitation!"

"I did so," Prudence said, looking up at Harry. "Why? I thought that since I am helping him with his memoirs he would make a useful ally."

Harry's expression was grim, his voice deadly, as he said, "You guessed wrong."

Prudence wanted to ask what he knew about the man that would cause her husband, the most amiable of men, to stiffen up in such a way, but she dared not. There were too many interested ears nearby and besides Lord Brandon was coming their way. She felt Harry's arm tighten on her waist.

"Colonel Langford," Lord Brandon greeted them with a bow. "And of course the lovely Mrs. Langford. May I take this opportunity to wish you both happy?"

"You are too kind," Harry said through gritted teeth.

"How nice of you," Prudence countered warmly.

Brandon bowed again. In a voice soft enough only to carry to their ears he said, "You may rest assured Colonel Langford that I do not plan to stay long. I confess I was surprised to receive the invitation and thought that it meant your family had, after all this time, decided to reconcile with mine. Patently I was mistaken."

"It was I who sent the invitation," Prudence confessed.

"That explains everything," Lord Brandon told her.

To Harry he added, "I shall take my leave as soon as I may do so without causing too great an amount of gossip. Nor shall I make such a mistake again."

"You are very good," Harry answered, but his voice was strained.

"Not at all," Brandon said with a nasty smile. "It is your wife who is very good to help me. I wonder, seeing your hostility now, that you let her."

Harry also smiled and his smile was equally unpleasant. "You should have realized, even upon such a short acquaintance, that my wife has a very strong will. Can you imagine anyone succeeding in telling her what she may or may not do?"

That surprised a bark of laughter out of Lord Brandon and he grinned at Harry. "I don't want to like you, Langford. But I confess that despite myself I do. And I shall therefore remove myself with all due speed. Good night. Mrs. Langford, I shall see you tomorrow. Or shall I?"

Prudence could feel Harry's hand on her waist. The tension in his body as he waited for her answer. She wanted to please him, but she could not. Not when so much was at stake. So in a voice that shook just a trifle, she said, "You shall see me tomorrow."

Lord Brandon bowed again and then moved away. Prudence could feel Harry beside her wanting to ring a peal over her head. No doubt he would do so later. But for now she refused to meet his gaze and instead pulled free to speak to someone she knew from before, someone who had known her uncle. Harry perforce had to follow.

She could feel his disapproval, and that of his brothers, without even looking at their faces. All of them seemed pointedly to ignore her from that point on. All except Sir Thomas Levenger, who managed to neatly cut her away from the other guests and draw her to one side.

"Here, my dear," he said handing her a glass of wine. "I should think you could use a restorative."

She looked up at him, a question in her eyes and he nodded. "Quite right," he said. "I do know what's wrong. And I am probably the only one in this room willing to tell you. But not here, not tonight. Come tomorrow and call upon my wife. I shall make it a point to stay home until noon. If you can manage to come before then I shall tell you all about it. Meanwhile, may I reassure you that otherwise you and Harry are doing very well tonight? You have both managed to carry the matter of your wedding off with great aplomb."

Prudence thanked him in a voice that was not altogether steady. He merely waved away her thanks with another smile and then managed to adroitly introduce her to someone who, as he put it, was likely to be quite sympathetic to a young woman with spirit and a taste for adventure. He was, as usual, absolutely correct.

Eventually the evening ended and everyone, including family, took their leave. The moment the last of the guests was gone, Lord and Lady Darton turned to Prudence.

"How dare you invite that man into our house?" Lord Darton demanded.

"I did not know how you would feel," Prudence said, surprised but pleased to hear that her voice did not tremble.

"Even if he were not who he is, why did you add a guest to the list without consulting me?" Athenia added, plainly puzzled.

Prudence blinked at her. "But you said I might invite a friend or two if I wished and that I need not trouble you with such details."

"You. Were. Mistaken." Lord Darton said, biting off each word.

Lady Darton, however, was more generous. "I did tell her so," she told her husband.

"Patently you should not have done so!"

"Surely we can discuss this in the morning?"

Athenia asked, trying once more to divert his anger. "I am certain we are all tired and should seek our beds."

"Nonsense!" Lord Darton countered. "I wish to have this settled now."

Athenia bit her lower lip. She looked at Prudence, standing with so pale a complexion in the middle of the room, and she looked at the anger on her husband's face. She made up her mind.

"George," she said, running a finger down his arm, "our bed. Don't you think we ought to seek our *bed*?"

As her meaning penetrated his angry temper, Lord Darton paused. He looked at Prudence. He looked at Athenia who smiled up at him winsomely. He looked back at Prudence and swallowed.

"Perhaps," he said in an oddly strained voice, "we should continue this discussion tomorrow."

And then he allowed himself to be drawn from the room. Which left Prudence and Harry alone together. There was no softness in his expression, none of the warmth she had come to expect, to need from him.

"Madam. I have long known you despise me for being a soldier. Until tonight I had no notion just how poor your taste in men might be. Good evening."

And then he turned to leave the room. Prudence could not help herself. She reached out to touch his arm. "Harry, please, tell me what was so very wrong about inviting Lord Brandon," she begged.

He merely stared at her with cold, harsh eyes until she removed her hand from his arm. "It does not matter," he said. "You have made your choice, and without even knowing the facts of the matter. My wishes, it appears, are immaterial to you. I only hope, Madam, that you can take some comfort in knowing you have won, for you shall have no other comfort of any sort from me."

Then, with head held high he started out of the room. Her voice stopped him.

"I see. I am to be condemned for acting without

knowing the facts. But you are noble because you do the same?"

He turned with surprising speed to face her. "I? Do the same? I think not!"

She advanced on him. "No? You condemn me for going to work for Lord Brandon without even stopping to consider that I may have excellent reasons of my own. You expect me to adopt your opinions and attitudes toward him without knowing a word of the reasons behind them. But I am to hold none of my own. After all, why should you think it matters? I am only your wife, not a real person."

Now his face was very, very pale. "You know that is not so," he said.

"No? Then prove it! Grant me the same trust you expect me to give you."

For several moments matters hung in the balance as they stared at one another, neither willing to give an inch. Finally it was Prudence who turned away. There was sadness in her voice, and a hint of defeat as well as she said, "You cannot, can you? Very well, I wish you joy of your pride and arrogance, Harry. And I hope you can find some comfort there for you will have none from me, either."

And then she strode from the room, brushing past Harry as if he were scarcely there. She took the stairs two at a time and pretended that she did not hear him call her name.

The maid was waiting to undress her and the moment her gown was undone she dismissed the woman so that she could be alone. It was all she could do to wait until the door closed behind her before she burst into tears. Her last thought as she did was that since meeting Harry she had turned into a veritable watering pot and cried more than in all the five years before that.

She half expected Harry to find a way to come to her, but he did not. She put on the night rail he liked the best, just in case. But still he did not come. And she waited, her hair fanned out on the pillow around her until the candle guttered low.

It was in the hours close to dawn that Prudence finally admitted to herself that he would not come, that they had gone too far tonight. It was the final straw and she quietly cried herself to sleep.

Chapter 19

Sir Thomas and Lady Levenger took one look at Prudence's face and guided her into a chair at the breakfast table. Orders were given for another place to be set and both plied her with coffee and food until she felt oddly comforted.

"You are very kind and I feel very foolish disturbing you so early," Prudence said with some constraint.

"Nonsense!" Sir Thomas said, waving his fork in her direction. "You showed great wisdom in coming at a time when you were likely to be given sustenance. The breakfast table in Lord Darton's house cannot have been a very comfortable one for you this morning, I'll be bound."

In spite of herself, Prudence smiled. "You may call it what you will but I am grateful." She looked down and then back at Sir Thomas. "You said, sir, that you know why the Langfords so strongly dislike Lord Brandon. Will you tell me?"

"It goes back to a time when the late Lord and Lady Darton were still alive," Sir Thomas said, setting down his fork and leaning forward. "Do you know anything about the late Lord Darton?"

"Harry told me he was a reformer. And that most of the *ton* ostracized him because of it."

"Quite right," Sir Thomas agreed. "What you have not heard, or you would never have invited him, is that Lord Brandon was among those who led the rest to turn their backs on Lord and Lady Darton. Worse, the Langfords believe it was he who spread certain unsavory rumors about Lady Darton. He knew, you see, that was what would hurt Lord Darton the most. There is no proof, you understand, but it is what the family believes. And the reason they do not welcome him in their homes."

"I see."

And she did. Prudence understood the full magnitude of her betrayal in the eyes of Harry and his family. "Why did no one tell me?" she asked Sir Thomas.

It was Lady Levenger who answered. "Even after all this time I would guess it still cuts to the quick. And they must have thought it would not be necessary."

Prudence nodded. She was silent for some moments. It was Sir Thomas who broke the silence. "Will you tell me," he said, "why it is that you chose to help Lord Brandon with his memoirs?"

He said it gently, amiably, as if it was a matter of mere curiosity. But there was a gleam in his eyes and the way he held himself taut as he waited for her reply that told Prudence there was much more to it than that.

"Will you mind if I tell you I cannot explain?"

"Yes."

One word. Spoken swiftly, with a brutal curtness that left no doubt he meant it. Prudence drew in a deep breath. "I have not even explained to Harry," she said, "but you are asking me to explain to you?"

"Yes."

This time the word came just as swiftly as before but with a hint of humor to the tone. She sighed and tilted her head to one side.

"You must be a very successful barrister," she said dryly.

"And you would make a very successful diplomat, if you were a man," he countered. "Come. It cannot be such a difficult question to require such prevarication. Unless, of course, you have something to hide? Some dishonorable secret that you dare not share."

He meant to provoke her and he almost succeeded. But even as Prudence opened her mouth to angrily refute the charge she stopped and laughed instead.

"No," she said, shaking her head. "You will not catch me out so easily." Then, soberly, meeting his eyes squarely so that he could not doubt that she meant what she said, Prudence told him, "My reasons are honorable. I am doing something I believe I must. It will, I hope, in the end be worth the anger Harry and his family now feel toward me. But the matter is so grave I cannot speak of it unless I am certain my suspicions are true."

"Then you are not fond of Lord Brandon?" Lady Levenger asked.

"No," Sir Thomas said, correctly reading her reaction, "Mrs. Langford is not. You greatly relieve my mind, my dear. Still, this is not a matter I can easily set aside. I have my own reasons for wishing to know. Reasons the Langfords do not even understand. Perhaps we should pool our knowledge and discover whether we might be of service to one another?"

Prudence regarded him warily. "Harry said you were a barrister. A justice who sits on the king's bench. Why, then, do I get the feeling you are much more than that?"

The corners of his eyes crinkled with amusement. "No doubt because I am," he said cordially.

"Thomas?" Lady Levenger said with some uncertainty.

The barrister reached out and patted his wife's hand. "It is all right, my dear. I consider myself an excellent judge of character and I believe I place myself in no jeopardy by saying what I have to Mrs. Langford. Do I?"

Fascinated, Prudence shook her head. "No, sir, you do not," she agreed.

"Perhaps not on purpose," Lady Levenger persisted, "but what if by accident she says the wrong thing to the wrong person? I do wish you would be more cautious, Thomas!"

"Well, Mrs. Langford, am I foolish to trust you?" he asked her.

"No," Prudence answered at once. "I am a diplomat's niece and a diplomat's daughter and I have moved in such circles almost all of my life. One learns early to hold one's tongue. You have honored me with your confidence and I shall not betray it."

"What? No promises? Simply a statement of fact?"

She had the sense he was teasing her. With a calm she was far from feeling Prudence replied, "Why should you believe words couched as a promise more than a simple statement of fact?"

He nodded, conceding her the point. "Enough prevarication. Come with me to my study and let us speak frankly of matters that are, I suspect, of great interest to both of us."

Lady Levenger watched them go with a worried look on her face and Prudence wished she could reassure her. But what could she say? Without knowing what Sir Thomas meant to tell her, she could see no way to do so.

Sir Thomas was all solicitude and waited until Prudence was seated before he spoke of the matter that had brought them there. "What do you hope to find out, working for Lord Brandon?" he asked.

Prudence regarded him with troubled eyes.

"If you are wondering," he added genially, "I know as much or more about the Langford family as any member in it. Though perhaps this is a matter that concerns your own family or honor instead?"

When she still hesitated he said, "Perhaps it would help if I tell you that there are concerns about Lord Brandon's loyalty?"

Prudence closed her eyes, then opened them again. "So it is not simply my imagination? I remember, you see, years ago often seeing him at parties in my uncle's home. He would speak quietly to people, one by one. I was young, too young to be at such parties though my uncle didn't seem to know it. At any rate, I was young enough so that no one ever seemed to take much notice of me or care what I might overhear. Lord Brandon said such odd things and when I tried to ask my uncle about them he told me I must have misunderstood."

"How many years ago?" Sir Thomas asked in a quiet voice that invited confidences.

"Perhaps ten or so. And other times since then."

He nodded. "Has Harry told you about a certain letter?" he asked carefully.

"When we were in France, there was trouble. Harry thought it would help to speak of a letter written, as he supposed, from Napoleon to his father. It seems he was mistaken for he only angered the Frenchman. He has not spoken of it again but it has stayed with me. I could not help thinking, you see, of the things I overheard Lord Brandon say and I wondered if it were perhaps he to whom the letter was written."

Sir Thomas let out a long breath. "I knew you were a shrewd woman!" he said. "Your thoughts march precisely in tune with mine. And I suppose you think to find out by working in Lord Brandon's study, helping him with his memoirs and hoping for a chance to go through his papers?"

Prudence smiled. "If we are to speak of shrewdness, sir, I should have to say that yours outruns mine. I have not told Harry what I intend because he has not spoken of the letter since that time in France. And because I know that I may be mistaken. But if you think I should then I will."

"Oh, no," Sir Thomas said, shaking his head emphatically. "I should like you to keep your counsel a while longer, if you can. There is more at stake than you realize."

"What is it you wish me to look for?"

Sir Thomas told her.

It was some time before Prudence left the Levenger's town house. Which meant that she was late arriving at Lord Brandon's home. He seemed more than a little surprised to see her.

"I thought you would not come today," he said bluntly.

Prudence unpinned her hat and set it aside and tossed her gloves on top before she answered. There was a hint of defiance in her voice and more than a little in the way she carried herself when she answered.

"I am not a china doll, sir, to be posed and set on the shelf. No, nor an empty-headed poppet to be told what to think or do. I have been accustomed to running my uncle's household and making my own decisions for many years now. It would be well for Harry—and his family—to realize this as soon as may be." She paused. Sir Thomas had warned her not to overdo the matter. In a lighter voice she said, "That is quite enough about me, sir. We have your book to write, my lord."

Brandon, who had been regarding Prudence with wariness now gave a shout of laughter. "I like a woman with spirit!"

He waved her to the writing desk where all the necessary materials stood ready. Still, it seemed he could not quite let the matter go and she was conscious that his eyes were regarding her sharply.

"Tell me," Brandon said, "am I to expect a visit from the colonel, demanding satisfaction for stealing his wife's affections from him?"

Again this was something she had discussed with Sir Thomas. So now Prudence merely raised her eyebrows and in a dampening tone replied, "I do not think my husband would wish to make so foolish a spectacle of himself. Nor can I imagine that he will be able to bring himself to set foot across your threshold. To work, my lord?"

Thus admonished, Lord Brandon had little choice

but to agree and they did, indeed, settle to work. It was when he was called out of the study to deal with a domestic crisis some time later that Prudence had her chance.

She was seated by the desk so as to better see the maps Lord Brandon was showing her. Thus she could open a drawer without being seen even had the door to the study been open. But it was not.

Lord Brandon's letters were neatly bundled and it took only a glance to see that it would not be easily done up in a hurry when she heard him return. She closed the drawer again then stood and walked over to the empty fireplace.

How odd, she thought. There were ashes there. Did his servants not clean the grate every morning? Prudence could not imagine that he would tolerate such slipshod practices in his house.

But perhaps he did not? With a pretense of having to sit to remove her shoe, Prudence sank into a chair beside the fireplace and looked more closely. The ashes were the remains of a letter. Perhaps more than one. She could read nothing but it was obvious that Lord Brandon had been destroying papers this morning before she arrived.

It occurred to Prudence that she might well be wasting her time looking for concealed letters or papers. Sir Thomas had certainly thought so. He had implied that more than once someone had been sent into the house as a servant to look and still found nothing. Perhaps he had been right that it would be better to see if she could draw Brandon out. She began to pace about the room, preparing her strategy.

That was how Lord Brandon found her. "Is something wrong, my dear?" he asked with great solicitude.

Prudence started. "I-I did not hear you return," she said.

He came toward her. "You look troubled," he said, peering at her closely. "Is something wrong?"

In a high, brittle voice Prudence laughed and tried

to turn the question away. "No, of course not. What could possibly be wrong? No, I am certain it is merely that I am unused to being married. Oh, but I should not have said even so much as that. I pray you will disregard it."

Had she overdone it? Lord Brandon tilted his head to one side. He indicated a chair. He hesitated before he spoke and Prudence held her breath. But she need not have worried. Brandon had taken the bait.

"Of course, my dear," he said. "If that is what you wish. But please, be seated. It is just that I should like to help, if I may, if you are troubled. You must know that I have a fondness for you."

Prudence put a hand to her throat. Again she looked away from him. "I, no, that is, there is no point to it. I am married and must make the best of it, that is all."

"All?" Brandon echoed. "Surely you chose to wed Colonel Langford? I am told it was a most romantic story."

He was skeptical. Well that was to be expected. Lord Brandon would not have survived so long if he were not a shrewd man. Prudence made herself laugh a harsh, brittle laugh.

"Of course that is the tale we told. What else was there to do?" she demanded.

If she appeared distracted, who could wonder at it? Or at the way she twisted the handkerchief in her lap.

Another pause. "Were you pressed to this marriage, then?" Brandon asked softly.

"I, what else was there to do?" Prudence repeated, more distracted than before. She appeared not even to see Lord Brandon as she spoke. "They said we were compromised. They said that time spent alone together meant we must be married. Everyone assured me he is an honorable man. He pretended to be kind."

"And he is not?" There was genuine disbelief in Brandon's tone. At her startled look he added, "I may dislike the Langfords and they me, but even I have never heard anything of such discredit to the colonel's character. He is said to be kind to a fault."

Prudence bit her lower lip. She had overplayed her hand and now she tried to retreat. She looked down at her lap. "Of course. Of course he is. I am being foolish. I pray you will disregard my nonsense."

But Brandon would not leave it be. "How has he been unkind? You need not fear to tell me, for I promise you I shall not let it go beyond this room."

Prudence lifted her eyes and looked straight into his, as though trying to gauge how truly he meant what he said. Finally she looked away. Her voice faltered as she tried to explain.

"You will think me foolish. Worse, a traitor! Harry does."

"Ah. A difference of political opinion, then?" Brandon asked, leaning forward, his gaze intense upon her face.

"I only meant that one should perhaps be prepared should Napoleon triumph. That one ought to consider how best to negotiate a way to ally ourselves with him in that event. But Harry calls me a traitor for saying so, for even suggesting such a thing."

Had she said too much? Gone too far? Prudence did not dare look at Lord Brandon to decide. He might read too much of her true feelings in her eyes. She had to play the role of the unhappy, meek wife who felt she did not know what she should do.

The silence stretched on and still he did not speak. Very well, it was up to her to take the next step. She rose to her feet and, still avoiding his eyes, she said, in a brisk voice, "I have shocked you. Pray forgive my foolishness. It was wrong of me and I shall not speak of it again. Now, where were we with your memoirs, Lord Brandon?"

She was moving toward the desk but he put out a hand to stop her. He was on his feet as well and looked down into her face searchingly. Prudence made herself stand very still. Apparently whatever he saw satisfied him for he seemed to relax.

"You are not the only one," he said with a small, tight smile, "who has had such thoughts."

Prudence looked at him doubtfully. "But Harry says I ought not to have them."

"Colonel Langford is a soldier," Brandon said kindly. "Naturally he would see this strictly in military terms of defeat and victory. We, who have lived in diplomatic circles more naturally think in terms of peace and compromise. Is that not so?"

As if reluctant, Prudence hesitated before she nodded. And she waited, as if afraid to speak. More and more of the tension in Lord Brandon's stance seemed to slip away. He moved to sit behind his desk and waved Prudence to the seat beside it. But instead of returning to his memoirs he steepled his fingers together, resting his elbows on the surface of his desk and looking at her with his piercing eyes.

"What would you think," he said, "if I told you that part of the trouble between the Langfords and myself has been over precisely such a difference in opinion?"

Prudence wanted to slap the man, so smug did he look. But Sir Thomas had impressed upon her how important this all was. She clasped her hands tightly together and looked down so that he would not see the contempt in her eyes.

"So that is why they were so upset with me for inviting you to Lord Darton's home? I am sorry they are so narrow-minded!" She reached out, as if impulsively, to put her hand over his. "It is not right," she said fiercely, "that they should blame you for having such common sense!"

Lord Brandon blinked at her, taken aback, and then began to .chuckle. "You've a temper, my dear. I had no notion of it. But how kind of you to use it in my behalf."

Prudence colored and withdrew her hand. "I-I am

sorry if I embarrassed you. I seem to be able to do nothing right today. Or indeed any day, of late."

Now it was he who patted her hand. "No, my dear, it is for me to apologize to you. I am neither distressed nor shocked nor even embarrassed. Indeed I am touched. I wonder what you would say if I were to ask a favor of you?"

"Anything!"

He smiled. "How impulsive of you. But perhaps it is because you are a good judge of character. As I consider myself to be."

Prudence nodded. "What is this favor, Lord Brandon?"

He regarded her with hooded eyes. With surprisingly little hesitation he explained.

"There was a time when I thought the late Lord Darton and I were friends. It seemed I was mistaken. He took a letter of mine. A letter I should very much like to have back. He would have returned it, I am certain he would, but he was killed in a carriage accident before he could do so. It was written in French. I thought that perhaps if you were to hear of such a letter, in the possession of the Langfords, that you could find and return it to me. It really is of no interest, nor concern, to anyone else. And it is mere spite that leads them to keep it from me."

"How terrible!" Prudence said sympathetically. "Do you have any notion where they keep it? Or what the date of the letter might be?"

"I have no notion where it is kept but the date is from some ten years past."

"I shall do my best," Prudence said warmly.

"Good. And now, my dear, back to work."

Chapter 20

Prudence went straight from Lord Brandon's town house to see Sir Thomas Levenger. He was not at home but Lady Levenger offered to let her write a note and promised to pass on Prudence's message the moment he returned.

Then Prudence went home. She hoped her maid would be sufficiently discreet not to mention either the earlier stop or this one to see Sir Thomas. At the woman's odd look, Prudence made herself laugh and say lightly, "I seem to be sadly shatter-brained today. I had promised Lady Levenger a recipe and when I stopped by this morning I forgot to give it to her."

The woman nodded but said not a word. Prudence stared out the carriage window wondering what Harry would say when he learned she had gone back to Lord Brandon's house today. And what the rest of his family would say as well.

But Harry was not home. He had left in something of a hurry, due to a message received from one of his brothers some time earlier. Prudence did not know whether to feel relieved or disappointed.

Philip, James, Harry, and Sir Thomas all stared at one another with dismay. And then they stared at the other man. Frederick Baines had taken a hand in a number of their projects and they knew him well enough to know that what he said mattered.

"Are you certain?" Harry asked.

Baines had a grim look about the mouth and eyes

as he replied, "I checked most carefully. Two men escaped. They were recaptured but they escaped again. Within weeks of their escape all communication ceased on the other side of the channel."

Sir Thomas took up the tale. "I've had a private communication. Wellington has received nothing from us for some time now. Nor can he spare a man to go and see what has happened. So for now we have no means of getting word over there."

"What do you suggest?" Philip asked.

Baines hesitated. "We must find out what is going on."

"Do you want me to go to France and see what is the matter?" James asked.

There was an immediate outcry against the notion. It was Philip who put their thoughts into blunt words. "Your French is execrable. You shouldn't last two minutes before you would be captured as a spy! Nor should I," he added to forestall James's natural protests. "If anyone were to go it must be someone better prepared than either of us."

"Quite right," Harry said quietly. "I shall go."

There was an even greater outcry at that. Particularly by James and Philip. Frederick Baines was the unlikely one who came to Harry's aid.

"I cannot like it," he said quietly, "but we must know. Do you truly think you are up to such a journey?" he asked Harry.

"Of course."

It was spoken with a degree of resolution that singularly failed to impress his brothers. Sir Thomas and Frederick Baines, however, regarded him thoughtfully. And then they looked at one another.

Sir Thomas said slowly, "I have never known Harry to fail at anything."

"He would be the best choice, if he were up to it," Baines agreed.

"Look, whether Harry goes or someone else, there

must be some reason you called Philip and me here as well," James pointed out, with some exasperation.

"Yes. Why did you wish to see all of us?" Philip added.

"Because," Sir Thomas said with a small smile, "we think you both can be of great use to us. Harry will either go or he will tell the man who does everything about the place where the signals were being received. You, Philip, can help plan some papers for Harry to carry that will seem to give him the authority to go where he wishes. I will translate them into French. And James, surely you must be able to think of some cunningly designed objects that would appear to be harmless but conceal things that would be of use to him?"

Sir Thomas knew the young men well. Within half an hour they were all deep in planning, writing notes for themselves or discussing possible notions between them. He watched, occasionally interjecting comments on, or objections to, the plans the men were making. This was, as he had known it would be, just the sort of project they would relish.

His only concern now was whether it was fair to let Harry go. He studied the younger man carefully, watching and trying to gauge how much pain his impassive expression might hide, how much his altered gait would slow him down should it come to a chase.

The boat rocked beneath his feet as Hugo Marland stared at the letter in his hands, all his attention taken by that simple piece of paper. He had read it more times than he could count and he still could not make sense of the fact that his niece had signed it Mrs. Langford. What the devil was she thinking, getting married like this, when he needed her?

And why couldn't she have sent the message sooner? As it was, it came too late for them to negotiate as they might have done had he known what was going on in Spain.

She'd been right about that. It was important. But not if it came too late. And why hadn't she brought it herself? This putative husband of hers, had he forbidden her to come? But didn't he understand how useful she was to him?

Lord Marland sighed. Selfish. That's what it was. Young men these days were remarkably selfish. No thought for anything save their own wishes. Well, he would be back in England soon and then he could speak to his niece and her husband in person. And try to discover what had happened to overset his plans so thoroughly.

A woman slipped her arm through his. She was of an age with him, petite and still possessed of a very fine figure. She smiled but he was hard put to smile back.

"How soon do we reach England?" she asked. "It has been far too many years and I am eager to see my daughter, Prudence."

Harry chose his moment carefully. He and Prudence were alone in the drawing room. And then he broke the news.

"I may have to go back to France."

"France? When? Why? The notion is absurd! You are not nearly recovered enough to do such a thing."

He ignored her cries of protest and took her hands in his, stroking the backs of them with his thumb. "I must," he said. "A great deal depends upon it. I cannot tell you why or even when, for certain. But soon."

She pulled her hands free and rose to her feet and began to pace about the room, shaking her head. "No, no. You cannot go. I will not let you. It is impossible. You are not well enough. Who would ask such a thing of you?"

With these last few words, this question, she rounded on Harry. He sat quietly, determined not to let her draw him into quarreling.

"I cannot tell you that either," he said.

"You cannot tell me," she echoed his words, her voice dripping with anger and sarcasm, "but you will go anyway. Despite what I might think, despite what I might say?"

"Yes. Just as you do what you wish, in the matter of Lord Brandon, without regard to my wishes."

She stared at him for a very long moment. Apparently she could see the determination in his eyes because suddenly she whirled and fled from the room. He did not try to follow. Words, he knew instinctively, would do no good. Perhaps after she had a chance to become accustomed to the shock. But not now, not yet. Nor was he certain, his anger over Lord Brandon still fresh, that he wished to reconcile with her.

George appeared to have overheard something of what occurred because he came softly into the room a moment later and took a seat opposite Harry. He cleared his throat. Twice. And then he spoke.

"So. You are going back to France. Did I hear correctly?"

Harry nodded and braced himself for a protest.

"I suppose you think it necessary?"

Harry nodded again.

It was George now who rose and paced about the room. He did not weep or cry out, but his grim expression betrayed his disapproval as clearly as anything Prudence had said or done. Finally he sighed heavily and turned to face Harry.

"I must suppose you know your own business better than I. And however foolish I might think such a step to be, I cannot forbid it. Still, I wonder."

"Well do not, I pray you," Harry snapped back. "I am only doing what I must do."

It was George's turn to nod. "Very well. What do you need and how can I help?"

Harry was taken aback at how quickly his eldest brother came to his support. And yet, it was the one quality he had always admired in George. His loyalty. Now his own voice was gruff with unspoken emotion as he said, "Take care of Prudence for me, while I am gone."

"As if you need ask!" George snorted. "Just do not ask me to keep her under control, for I will not even try. But she shall have a home with us for as long as necessary."

Harry smiled despite himself and despite the circumstances that brought him to this point. "I do not ask the impossible, George. If you take care of her, give her a home, I shall not ask more of you than that."

George came to sit opposite Harry again. "Can you tell me anything of why you are going to France?"

Harry shook his head.

"I did not think so. I suppose I am not to mention it to anyone, either?" he hazarded shrewdly.

Harry looked at his brother with newfound respect, at which George snorted. "I am not the fool you and your brothers sometimes take me for. I know you have often been involved in rather, shall we say, unusual circumstances. Aye, and involved your brothers as well. No," he said holding up a hand to forestall Harry's instinctive protest, "don't tell me anything. I do not need to know. I simply wish to make certain I do not place you in danger by saying the wrong thing to the wrong person at the wrong moment."

Harry grinned at George. "You are an excellent fellow!" he exclaimed.

Lord Darton grinned back. "I am delighted you think so. Now tell me how I can help you."

Harry placed a few commissions with George. And pretended he did not see how the lines of worry on his brother's face increased as he did so. In a way, he was not surprised that George did not simply let the matter drop.

"Harry, I should not presume to tell you your business."

Harry quirked an eyebrow but George ignored him and pressed on.

"I wonder, though, if you are pushing yourself to do this because of Father."

"Father?" Harry demanded, taken aback.

"Yes, Father. I have noticed we all tend to do things because of him. I have a horror of anyone taking me for a reformer, for example."

"Impossible!"

George gave him a withering look. "Philip pursues the law because he wants to help without appearing to be the odd creature Father was. And James, well, the less said about the difference between the careless face he presents the world and his true vocation inventing things the better."

Harry sat straight upright at that. "You know about his inventions?"

Again that withering look. "I am not a complete fool even though I know that you and James and Philip sometimes take me for one. I know and understand a great deal more than any of you give me credit for. The thing is, Harry, I wonder if we have not all made a mistake."

"A mistake?" Harry echoed warily.

"Yes, a mistake. We have tried so hard to distance ourselves from Father and who and what he was that we have lost sight of the things to be admired about him. We have traded away pieces of ourselves so that none will mistake us for him. I sometimes think you went into the military because you wanted to prove that we are a loyal family, that we are honorable. But it is time to have done with such things! It is time to accept who we are and the ways in which we are like Father as well as the ways we are different."

George paused and Harry tried to marshal his rattled thoughts. He proceeded with great caution as he asked, "Even you, George?"

"Even me. I am discovering that perhaps Athenia and I ought not, perhaps, to be quite so rigid in the way we live our lives. That perhaps we have traded away something important to do so."

Harry could only gape at his brother, a circumstance that seemed to amuse George greatly. He even laughed.

"You need not look as though I have grown several heads," George chuckled. "I merely wish you to understand that you ought to think through this venture most carefully. It is not that I doubt your ability to do what you must, but are you certain it would not be better for someone else to go in your place? Are you certain it is not vanity or pride or a need to still prove yourself that causes you to insist upon this step?"

He paused then stared Harry straight in the eyes as he said, "You see, as much as I admire you and your skills, I cannot believe that there is no one in all of England who could do the job as well or better than you. No, you need not answer me now. Indeed, you need not answer me at all. You need only answer yourself. Good night, Harry. I shall leave you to your thoughts. Athenia is waiting for me upstairs."

And then, with a wink, George quitted the room. It was some time before Harry could collect his wits sufficiently to shut his mouth and consider what his brother had said. It annoyed him greatly to discover that there was more than a grain of truth to it. And that he, himself, was feeling a few niggling doubts over what he meant to do. Harry did not like doubts.

Chapter 21

Harry avoided Prudence the next day. And George. As much as he disliked to admit it, his brother's words nagged at him and there was a tiny voice in his head that did indeed wonder if he was being unbearably arrogant in assuming that he was the best one, the only one who could undertake this task.

And yet he had given his word. Confused but determined, Harry set off early for Philip's town house where he found James and Philip and Sir Thomas and Frederick Baines already there. They showed no signs of the doubts George had planted in his head and Harry could not, he found, bring himself to share them with these men. Instead, he threw himself into the planning as if he had no doubts that he would be going. He carefully did not let himself think about how Prudence must be feeling.

Emily and Juliet, accustomed to this sort of thing and suspecting that Prudence was not, rallied around her. They called to take her shopping with them, even though she was reluctant.

"You cannot, you really cannot continue to wear those dresses," Emily told her firmly. "It was kind of Athenia to have her old gowns made over for you but they are now unfashionable and entirely too dull!"

"You will like Mrs. Wise. She has an excellent eye and will know precisely what will suit you," Juliet added.

"I know what suits me," Prudence countered, a militant gleam in her eyes.

"To be sure, of course you do," Emily agreed in a soothing voice. "But Mrs. Wise may have some notions you have not thought of. Nor will it cost you a fortune, as it would if Athenia were to take you to her modiste."

"Besides it will give us a chance to talk with you about Harry and George and Athenia," Juliet chimed in.

Prudence stared at them. "Why," she asked grimly, "didn't you simply say so in the first place? Of course I shall go with you then. But there is no need to visit a modiste."

Emily looked at Prudence's gown. "Oh, yes, there is," she countered. "That may have been in fashion when Athenia purchased it, but it most assuredly is no longer so. Nor would it ever have truly suited you."

This was a charge Prudence could not refute so she gave in with a sigh. When had she stopped caring about her clothing? There was a time when it was one of the uppermost thoughts in her mind, because she understood the value of appearance in her dealings with the men where her uncle was posted. There was a time when the placement of a ribbon or the removal of a row of ruching might mean the difference between her uncle prevailing in talks or failing and she had known it. But somehow, since she had returned to England with Harry, she had scarcely given a second thought to her clothes. Perhaps it was as well that these two women were taking her in hand.

Mrs. Wise had no shop. Instead she worked from her home. It was in a somewhat better location than when Emily had first taken Juliet there to order her clothes, but still Prudence felt a pang of nervousness as they entered the building under the watchful gaze of far too many envious women and children. Why the devil, she wondered, would her sisters patronize such an unfashionable location as this?

But Mrs. Wise herself was dressed neatly and attractively, as were the girls who worked for her. Juliet greeted one by name and with a great degree of warmth. Emily explained their errand and drew Prudence forward. Within minutes Prudence and Mrs. Wise were friends. It was a perfectly natural circumstance given that both women had an excellent eye for form and color and a shrewd understanding of the purpose to which clothing could be put.

By the time they left, Prudence was in a fair way to forgiving her sisters for abducting her in such a way. She had no objection when they took her to purchase gloves and slippers and so forth to go with the dresses she had just ordered. She felt a moment's pang at the cost but both Juliet and Emily assured her the charges were most reasonable and, if they did prove too dear for Harry's pocketbook, they would both make a present of the cost to Prudence. She could not refuse without looking most ungracious. Nor did she complain when they suggested a drive about the park. It was only when they wanted to discuss Harry that she drew the line. But it was hard to stay angry.

"It is only natural you should object to our asking," Emily assured her warmly.

"And we would not do so if we were not so fond of him," Juliet added.

"But after this afternoon we are fond of you as well," Emily made haste to say.

"Yes, we should now like to see your marriage succeed for both your sakes," Juliet concluded.

"I ought," Prudence said in a judicious tone, "to ask the coachman to stop so that I could get down and walk home. But I shan't," she added, at their look of alarm. "I know you mean well. And, to be honest, I should be glad of some advice. Harry is not at all happy about Lord Brandon and while I cannot stop helping the man with his memoirs I should be grateful for suggestions as to how to turn Harry up sweet. There is a particular reason I should like him not to wish to leave me alone just now."

Juliet and Emily looked at one another, then at Prudence, then at each other again.

"The book," they said as one.

"Book?" Prudence echoed cautiously.

"The book," they repeated.

"I think," Emily said, "we had best go around to my house and there Juliet and I can show you a most useful book I found in my husband's library."

Intrigued, Prudence made no objection. After all, she liked books. She could not see how one could help her marriage, but neither could she see any harm in looking at it.

A short time later the three ladies were ensconced in Philip's library. The book was open, held by Prudence sitting between Emily and Juliet. Her eyes were wide as she turned the pages and the other two ladies pointed out their favorite pictures.

At one point she turned the book first one way, then the other, then asked, doubtfully, "Do you think that position is truly possible?"

And why Juliet and Emily should laugh at the question was beyond Prudence. But after a moment they sobered and Juliet explained, "We said precisely the same thing the first time we saw that picture. We have not yet figured out a way to manage it but it must be possible or surely they would not have put it in the book."

Prudence looked at Emily enquiringly and she blushed. "I have not yet had the courage to suggest it to Philip," she admitted. "And it does look most improbable."

Prudence looked from one to the other. "So you really have used what you found here?" she asked.

They both nodded. Prudence was silent for a very long moment and then she turned her attention back to the book. "I think," she said, "you might have a point."

Prudence found herself verbally fencing with Lord Brandon each day. It was as though he wished to determine her precise feelings about the family. And he pressed her for the letter. Sir Thomas wished her to encourage Lord Brandon but was adamant that the actual letter should not fall into the man's hands again. But he had a copy made. Not precisely the same as the original, but Sir Thomas felt that after ten years, the man would be unlikely to recollect so precisely that he would notice. This he gave to Prudence. Lord Brandon was delighted when she gave him the letter. Something gleamed in his eyes that frightened her, but he was careful to swiftly hide it again. And then he turned his attention to her.

"Are you happy, my dear?" he asked with grave solicitude. "Are you more at ease with Colonel Langford's family yet?"

Prudence quirked a wry smile. Harry was avoiding her. He still, so far as she could tell, meant to go back to France and he still would not tell her why. So it was no great difficulty to look away from Lord Brandon and shake her head as though too distressed to speak.

Then, as Sir Thomas had predicted he would, Lord Brandon began to reveal himself a little more. "I beg you will confide in me, my dear," he said. "I cannot believe they are entirely kind to you or that it is an establishment which truly suits you. Perhaps there is a way in which I can help."

Prudence chose her words with great care. "I cannot see how, Lord Brandon. But you are right, I am not entirely happy in Lord Darton's household. I suppose you shall think me more shallow even then you already do, but I am accustomed to presiding over my uncle's establishment. Accustomed to playing hostess to diplomatic parties and such. Here I am relegated to the status of a poor relation. I cannot believe I have come to such a pass. My future stretches out before me like one very long nightmare."

Prudence broke off and looked at him, letting Lord Brandon see the full measure of her current misery in her eyes. Then, she looked away, down at the floor as she said, "But I ought not to burden you with my troubles. No, nor give you a worse opinion of me. It is the megrims, that is all. I shall be fine, directly, I assure you."

He came around the desk, as she knew he would, and took her hands. Prudence had to force herself neither to flinch nor to pull her hands free. This was important, she told herself. And so she merely swallowed hard and kept looking at the floor. She even stood still when he tilted up her chin to make her look at him.

"I do not think you shallow. Nor selfish. Nor any other evil thing you are thinking about yourself," he said softly. "I think you a courageous young woman caught up in circumstances she does not deserve."

Now Prudence allowed herself to pull her chin free. She took a deep breath and said, "That is as may be. But these are my circumstances and I must make the best of them."

"Perhaps. Perhaps not."

She stared at him. "But how could they be altered?" she asked with a bewildered air.

Brandon turned and walked away from her. He stood for some moments staring out the window of his study, his back to her. Then, abruptly, he whirled around. "What if," he said softly, "your husband could inherit the title?"

A laugh of disbelief burst out of Prudence, entirely uncalculated. "That is absurd!" she said, not needing to playact now. "Lord Darton has sons."

"What if they were to all disappear. Pouf! All in one moment?" Brandon persisted.

Prudence froze. The man could not possibly be saying what she thought he meant, could he? For a moment she forgot the role she was playing and anger blazed out of her eyes. He took a step backward in alarm and Prudence hastily recollected the role she had promised Sir Thomas she would play.

She let a spark of hope appear in her expression

before her shoulders dropped, as though in defeat. "That is scarcely likely to happen. No, nor should I wish for it either, even if I could. I must look instead to accustom myself to the reality of my circumstances. Somehow I shall. I must."

This last was said fiercely and Brandon came closer again. He put a hand on her shoulder. "Perhaps not," he said. "Tell me. Do you think you could arrange some sort of expedition? Perhaps out to the country-side? Or Astley's Amphitheater? Or any such thing? The entire family? Even the younger brothers and their wives? And could you contrive to be in a carriage of your own with just your husband beside you?"

"I-I suppose I could," Prudence said slowly. "But to what point?"

Brandon hesitated, then seemed to make up his mind. "It has happened before," he said carefully, "that carriage accidents occurred. With no one the wiser. Who is to say it could not happen again? Think of it: not one Langford left to harass you!"

Prudence held her breath. It was both part of the act she played and to allow herself a moment to think for her thoughts were all a whirl and she did not think she could have answered Lord Brandon coherently, even if she wished to do so.

Finally, when he seemed to grow a trifle impatient, she said carefully, "Where and when and how would such a journey need to be arranged?"

Lord Brandon gave a tiny crow of laughter. "I knew I could not be mistaken in you," he said. "Why don't we say a week hence. You can tell me the precise day and time the moment you know it and I shall arrange everything else."

Prudence made herself put out a hand and touch his sleeve. If it trembled, why so much the better. It lent verisimilitude to her part.

"It will not be dangerous, will it?"

He put his hand over hers and smiled a smile that

reminded Prudence of nothing so much as a snake. "Not at all," he assured her. "Not at all."

He waited for her to nod then let go of her hand and moved briskly away from her and back behind his desk. "Very well. Now that we have that matter settled, shall we get back to work?"

Prudence took the chair he indicated and set to work as though they had not just plotted the murder of Harry's entire family. Nor did her expression betray one bit her impatience to go to Sir Thomas and tell him everything. He had told her he thought Lord Brandon might make such an offer but Prudence had not believed him. Now she did and it chilled her to the bone.

Was this what had happened to the late Lord and Lady Darton? And could Sir Thomas protect the current family? He had said to listen to whatever plan Lord Brandon proposed. He had said not to refuse anything, no matter how outrageous. But still, perhaps she had agreed to this too hastily. Perhaps she ought to have spoken with Sir Thomas first.

Prudence made herself take a deep breath. She would talk to Sir Thomas as soon as possible. She could always refuse, after all, to arrange the trip. And then Lord Brandon would have no handy target. But if it were possible, she thought, she would prefer to have Brandon neatly caught at what he meant to do. For as long as the man walked free, she did not think she would draw an easy breath again.

Chapter 22

No one, seeing the two figures entering the elegant hotel, Grillon's, in London would have guessed at the importance of either one. The woman was petite, with excellent features, but they were scarcely visible, so closely did she keep her hooded cloak clasped about her.

As for the gentleman, he was in no way remarkable to look at. To be sure, he spoke in a fine, mellifluous voice, but he was not above-average height, his shoulders not overly broad, and his face was quite forgettable.

Still, upon hearing the name of Marland, the staff of Grillon's was instantly obsequious. A set of rooms was found to be available. Orders were given and the two shown to what would be their home here in London for at least the next week or two.

Only when they were alone did the lady remove her cloak and toss it on the nearest chair. One of the servants could take care of it later.

"It is good to be back in London," she said with a happy sigh.

"It won't be so pleasant if anyone gets wind of who you are," her companion countered. "Or worse, of where you have been all these years."

She leaned her head against the back of the elegantly upholstered sofa. There was a mischievous grin on her face as she said, "Perhaps I should tell the truth and let the scandal fall where it may."

He recoiled then leaned forward. "Don't even jest

about such a thing," he told her, his voice urgent, "or I shall wash my hands of you entirely! Don't you comprehend how dangerous it could be?"

She shrugged. "I did not come back to England to hide. But very well," she said, holding up a hand to forestall his evident protests, "we shall do it as you wish. For the moment."

He let out a deep sigh and did not even trouble to try to hide his relief. "It will be for the best."

"Perhaps. But you had best find a way for me to see her, and soon."

The man bowed. "I shall call upon her today."

"Now."

He hesitated. He wanted to argue, but there was no point. "Let me change and I shall be on my way."

Half an hour later, he knocked on the front door of Lord Darton's town house. When he handed in his card he was admitted at once and taken to the drawing room. A lady greeted him, but not the one he was seeking.

"Hello Lord Marland, I am Lady Darton. I am very sorry your niece is not here. Unfortunately she is a trifle headstrong and cannot seem to bring herself ever to stay home."

"Will she be back later?" he persisted.

Lady Darton gave a very dainty and very eloquent shrug. "I cannot say, sir. I would like to think so. But of late she spends a great deal of time with Lord Brandon."

"Lord Brandon!" Hugo Marland was taken aback.

With a hint of maliciousness in her smile Lady Darton said, "Why don't you ask for her there? At the very least, even if she is not there, no doubt his lordship will know when she is expected. However careless she is with us, with family, I collect she is much more responsible with him."

"Thank you," Lord Marland said, bowing to Lady Darton, his thoughts still in a whirl.

Lord Brandon! Of all people, he would never have expected her to strike up a friendship with him. And didn't her husband object? Of all the reports he had heard of the man, Colonel Harry Langford was not a man to suffer fools or traitors lightly.

Lord Marland said none of this aloud. Instead he bowed again, said a few gracious words, then took his leave. On the street he paused to consider. But in the end he could see no better choice than to do as Lady Darton suggested. He signaled a passing hackney and directed the driver to take him to Lord Brandon's town house. Perhaps here he would have some answers.

Lord Brandon certainly greeted him affably enough. "When did you return to London? I thought you had been sent to the talks on the continent."

Lord Marland turned his hand this way and that. "I shall have to go back, of course, but I wished to come and see about my niece's wedding to Langford. I called at Lord Darton's house but she was not there and I was told that perhaps she might be here."

Brandon offered his guest a glass of brandy and as he handed it to him, studied the man carefully. At last he said, "She is not expected until sometime later, I'm afraid."

Marland smiled his innocuous smile. The one that led so many to underestimate him. "Good! Then you can tell me how she is doing without fearing we shall be interrupted by her unexpected entrance."

Brandon blinked in surprise, then he shrugged and laughed. "Why not?" he said, as much to himself as to Marland "What do you wish to know?"

"How is she? Is she happy? Anxious? Does this Colonel Langford treat her well? Why the devil did she marry him, anyway?"

Even as he spoke them, Lord Marland realized how dearly he wanted answers. Not polite assurances, but some real understanding of Prudence's circumstances.

For a moment he thought Lord Brandon might refuse to answer and then the man began to talk.

"She is very brave, your niece. She tells the world she is content with her marriage, but I am not altogether certain she is telling the truth. Still, it was her choice and I do not see how anyone can alter matters for her. As for why she married him, did she not tell you? She and Colonel Langford wandered about France for a couple of months together, unchaperoned. And when they finally reached Wellington's lines, the great man himself ordered them to be married because he felt Langford had hopelessly compromised your niece's reputation. They put it about, once they returned to London, that it was a love match but I can assure you that I have observed the pair closely enough to be certain that it was not."

This was not what Lord Marland wanted to hear. He gripped his glass tighter. "I see. And now she is helping you write your memoirs?"

Lord Brandon spread his hands wide. "I offer her a diversion for her thoughts, and a small recompense that no doubt supplements whatever pin money the impecunious colonel can spare her. Indeed, I like to think that my home may be a sort of refuge for her."

Marland regarded the other man for several long moments. Then, slowly, unsteadily, he rose to his feet. "I thank you for that," he said, his voice a trifle harsh with emotion. "And now I know you will excuse me. I must be going."

"Come again. Any time," Lord Brandon told him, walking Lord Marland to the door of the study.

And then he was out in the street again, trying to hail another hackney. His head was in a whirl, trying to sort out the truth in what Brandon had told him. But it was impossible. He would simply have to go back to the hotel, relate everything he had been told, and let her sort out what she wished to believe.

So intent was he on his thoughts that he didn't even

see the private carriage come to a halt scarcely a few feet away from him.

"Uncle?" a soft voice called out. Then, louder, "What are you doing here? Were you calling upon Lord Brandon? How long do you have before you are posted out again?"

In spite of himself, Marland laughed. Prudence had always had the trick of making him do that. "I am looking for you. Lady Darton thought I might find you here. How are you, my little puss?"

She smiled up at him and slipped her arm through his. "I am a married woman now and you must treat me with respect, Uncle."

"I have always treated you with respect," he countered, with a chuckle. "You taught me the folly of not doing so some years ago." He stepped back and looked at her. "You look happy," he said.

"Now why do you sound surprised?" Prudence asked. "Have you been listening to gossip? Very foolish of you."

"Ma'am? They are holding the door open for us," a woman, obviously a maid, told Prudence and Lord Marland.

"Come in," Prudence said coaxingly. "I shall give my regrets to Lord Brandon and tell him I shall come back another day. Then we may go back to Lord Darton's town house, or to wherever you are staying, and have a comfortable coze together."

"No, no," he said abruptly. "You go and help his lordship with his memoirs. I shall call upon you tomorrow morning."

"I am not going anywhere," she said with that determined glint in her eyes that he knew meant trouble, "until you tell me where you are staying."

With a sigh, Lord Marland replied, "Grillon's."

Now she was all smiles again. "Good. I shall see you there later."

Then, with a kiss for his cheek, she hurried up the steps followed by the maid, who cast him doubtful and disapproving glances. But that was the least of his troubles. He was going to have to go back to Grillon's and tell his sister-in-law that Prudence was on her way. He shuddered at the thought of what her reaction was going to be.

Chapter 23

Prudence paused as she entered Grillon's. She smoothed down her skirts and then glanced at her maid who, stiff with disapproval, accompanied her into the hotel.

"They will be expecting us back home," she said with a sniff.

"To be sure, they will," Prudence replied. "Which is why I think you should go back and tell them where I am. I am certain my uncle will escort me home later."

"Once I see you safely upstairs," the maid answered, determined to observe the proprieties even if her mistress did not.

The door opened and Prudence was shown in to where her uncle and a woman sat talking. They both rose at the sight of her. Prudence immediately turned to the maid.

"There. You see? My uncle is here and I am perfectly safe. Now you can go home and I shall see you there later. My uncle will escort me and it will all be perfectly unexceptionable."

"Yes, ma'am," the maid replied, sounding almost disappointed there was to be no scandal involved.

The woman retreated and all three people in the room remained silent until she was gone. Then Prudence turned to her uncle and smiled warmly.

"My apologies. I am hemmed about with restraints these days. No one seems to be able to conceive that I might be able to manage on my own despite the fact that I have been doing so for years. How are you, Uncle? You must tell me all about the talks on the continent and why you have returned early. But first I pray you will introduce me to your guest."

And why that simple request should cause her uncle to color up and stammer was beyond Prudence. She looked at the woman, trying to fathom her uncle's odd reaction.

The woman was smiling and there was something oddly familiar about her. It took Prudence several moments to realize what it might be.

"Mother?"

The woman beamed. "There. I told you, Hugo, that she would recognize me! My dear, how are you?"

"But you're dead!"

The woman laughed. A warm, rich laugh that reminded Prudence of a time, so many years ago, when she would hear that laugh and know she was safe and loved. A time when she thought she would have her mother forever. When she trusted her mother.

"Why?" she asked, pulling back when the woman would have hugged her. "Why? Why did you go? Where did you go? Why did you let me believe you were dead?"

Prudence looked for signs of guilt, for signs that she regretted leaving her child, but there were none. The woman was entirely composed. She raised her eyebrows, as though Prudence were the one who had offended.

"Did you think my life revolved around you?" the woman asked. "That I had no other obligations?"

Prudence flinched. "And my father?" she asked, her voice cold. "Is he alive as well?"

Now regret crossed her mother's face. And sadness tinged her reply. "No. He died when you thought I did. When I did almost die."

The woman reached out and took Prudence's hand, ignoring her efforts to pull free. "Come. Sit. You deserve to know the truth of what occurred."

"A few years too late!" Prudence countered, but she sat down beside her mother.

"Perhaps. But there were reasons for it. Lives were at stake. Including mine. It was more than ten years ago. Napoleon was not yet in power, but he already knew he was going to be. Your father and I were in France. Unofficially, of course, you understand. We suspected it might not be entirely safe and that is why we left you with Hugo."

Her mother paused and drew in a deep breath. "Unfortunately, we were right. One night there was a mob. Your father and I were caught up in it. We were both beaten. He died. I didn't. But it took me months to recover. Even more to be glad I was still alive. The Frenchman who took me in was not yet powerful. But he would be. What he was, was kind. He helped me to recover, he helped me to find a way out of my grief for your father."

"And so you became his wife?" Prudence asked. "No wonder you could not tell me, could not tell anyone. You would have been called, we all would have been called, traitors."

"It was worse than that," her uncle interjected. "Your mother didn't become his wife, she became his mistress."

Prudence stared at her mother in disbelief. Her mother looked away and shrugged, though Prudence guessed that careless gesture cost her mother dearly.

"He was already married. There was no choice, not if I wanted to stay with him. And there were reasons for me to do so. Reasons of state. Already it was evident he would have the ear of Napoleon, he would have power. And I would be able to send information back to England. Not easily and it would be dangerous, but no one else was in the position I was to help."

"And what about me?"

Prudence sounded petulant. She could hear it in her voice, but she could not stop herself. What were matters of state to a young girl on the brink of womanhood? What were matters of state to a child who needed her mother?

She must have spoken out loud. Or perhaps her mother had asked herself the same questions over the years. In any case, she answered.

"I knew you were safe with Hugo. I knew he would take care of you. By the time I was recovered enough so that I could have returned, a great deal of time had passed. I thought that perhaps you would have become accustomed to my death by then and it would be more difficult for you if I did return."

Prudence spoke the worst oath she had heard while in France. Her mother flinched.

"Maybe I was wrong," she said. "But I had to stay. I had to do what I did."

Prudence took a deep breath and tried to comprehend everything. "Why would Napoleon have trusted a man whose mistress was English?" she demanded abruptly.

"Few knew I was his mistress. And none of those knew who I was. I told him, told everyone, that I was from the American colonies. Which is true, you know. I told him I had no real love for England, that my father had been killed by the British. Which was also true. I met your father when he was posted to the colonies and I fell in love with him despite the fact that he was British. And so they trusted me."

Prudence rose and paced about the room. Over her shoulder she flung accusations at her mother. "What about the principles with which you raised me? Your belief that war was abhorrent? That one must avoid it at all costs? Patently you have helped to keep this one' going by passing on information as you did."

Her mother came, took her by the shoulders, and looked her squarely in the eyes. "I did what I had to do. What I believed would save lives. And what would protect England and other countries from the horrors I saw in France. To believe in peace is wonderful. Perhaps some day it will even be a reality, that we need not have war. But that day has not yet come. And reality taught me that sometimes one must look beyond principles."

"You sound," Prudence replied, not troubling to hide the bitterness in her voice, "like Harry. He says the same and plans to go back to France. Injured as he is I cannot think but that he is throwing his life away."

Instead of taking offense, as Prudence half-expected her to do, her mother drew her back over to the sofa and pulled her to a seat.

"Tell me about Harry," she said gently.

Prudence did so. Perhaps it was not wise, perhaps it was not discreet, but she did so. And when she was done, there was a troubled look on her mother's face. Prudence tried to change the subject.

"Why come back now?" she demanded.

"To see you."

That might have warmed Prudence's heart had her uncle not added dryly, "The man whose protection your mother was under is dead. That may have played a part in her decision. Especially since she might have come under suspicion as having had a hand in his death."

Prudence looked sharply at her mother but the woman only shook her head. "All nonsense. No one really suspected me. They knew it was his wife. Still, it seemed a good time to travel to where the talks were being held."

"To meet my uncle," Prudence said slowly.

"Yes. And then come home to see you!" her mother said triumphantly.

"But do you mean to stay?"

Her uncle rubbed the side of his nose. "Well, there is a problem with that. Everyone thinks your mother dead. Should she suddenly reappear, it would be a tremendous scandal and word would get back to France. That would undo a great deal of useful work, you see."

"I plan to go on to America, if we can find a ship

that will take me there, by some roundabout route," her mother explained. "But I had to see you first."

Prudence did not answer her mother but looked, instead, at her uncle. "How long have you known she was alive?"

He did not at once answer and his silence told Prudence all she needed to know. "Why didn't you tell me?" she asked, softly.

"You were a child," he said impatiently. "We could not trust you not to tell. Or to give yourself away by your happiness if you knew she was alive."

"I would not have done so," Prudence said stiffly.

Even as she said the words, she wondered if they were true. Would she have demanded her mother? Told her friends? In some way betrayed the secret? Perhaps put her mother, and others, at risk?

She sighed. "How long do you mean to stay in London, mother?" she asked.

A shrug. "It will not be easy to arrange passage. Not with the war going on between England and the United States. It may take some time to arrange or I might be gone by next week."

Prudence sat beside her mother and took her mother's hands in her own. "Then we have no time to lose, do we?"

Harry stared out the window. Over his shoulder he said, "Her uncle? Are you certain?"

Lady Darton's voice was sympathetic as she replied, "Her maid was most adamant on that point. And even if it were not, there was a woman present to serve as chaperon."

"I see."

Lord Darton clapped his brother on the shoulder. "So she did not tell you that her uncle was coming back so soon. Perhaps she didn't know. The maid said she seemed surprised to find him outside Lord Brandon's house."

Harry turned to look at his brother. "And why the devil was he there?"

Lady Darton colored up but he didn't see her. Still, he heard her voice as she said, "I fear I am responsible. I sent Lord Marland there to see her."

Some of the tension seemed to go out of Harry's shoulders. He could not have said precisely why he was disturbed by the notion of Lord Brandon and Lord Marland together, but he had been. Particularly after Prudence had championed Lord Brandon already.

As though summoned by his thoughts, there was a stir in the doorway and he turned to find Prudence standing there, her face pale but with two bright spots of red on her cheeks. Without stopping to think he went toward her.

"What's wrong?" he asked taking her hands.

They were shaking, he realized, and he drew her to him, enfolding her in his embrace, oblivious to George and Athenia behind him. Suddenly all his past anger at her seemed unimportant. All that mattered was that she needed him.

"What's wrong?" he repeated softly to the top of her head.

She looked up at him. There was pain in her eyes and her voice trembled as she said, "My uncle is back in London."

"And isn't that a good thing?" he teased, bewildered by her reaction. "I thought you liked the fellow."

"I do, but—"

She looked beyond him and Harry heard George clear his throat.

"Er, perhaps you and Prudence would care to talk matters over in your room, Harry?"

"Er, yes, of course," Harry said. "Come, my dear. We shall be more private there."

She came without a word of objection and that lack of temper, of spirit alarmed Harry more than anything else could have done. Wilkins took one look at the pair and excused himself.

Harry drew Prudence to the bed and undid her bonnet. He drew off her gloves and set them down on a chair. Only then did he tip up her chin to make her look at him.

"What's wrong?" he asked yet again.

Chapter 24

Prudence stared up at Harry. What was she to tell him? Her uncle and mother had both impressed upon her the need for secrecy and she could well understand it herself. And yet how could she not tell Harry? Especially since her mother's words still haunted her. About honor and duty and the need to work to protect others. She would have to tell Harry that she understood his need to go back to France and yet she was desperately afraid to do so.

And if she did not tell him any of this, then what was she to say to him? She opened her mouth to pass it off lightly with a jest and misdirection and realized she could not lie to this man. Not now, not ever.

He was so earnest and he looked at her with such concern in his eyes. All he wanted to do was comfort her but how could she let him? And yet how could she not? These past days, when he looked at her with such anger in his eyes had been unbearable. She could not risk going back to such a state of affairs between them.

Abruptly Prudence drew in a deep breath. She would not tell Harry, but neither would she lie. And the moment this was all over, she would do whatever it took to bring him to this point again.

"I-I pledged my uncle I would not speak of any of what he told me," she stammered. "Not even to you, though I dearly wish I could. I-I know you must find that unforgivable, so I will go."

But he would not let her go. Instead he caught her

hands and held them gently but implacably. "If you have given your word," he said, "then of course you must keep it. But that does not mean you must run from me. Or from the comfort I would give you. Whatever is distressing you, don't you think it is both my right and my obligation to offer you what help I can?"

And what was there to say to that? How could she object when he was smiling at her so kindly? When he held her hands with such gentleness and looked at her with such warmth in his eyes? How could she be so foolish as to refuse what she so dearly needed? And he was so willing to give?

So now she let him draw her to him. And of her own accord she tilted up her chin to meet his gaze. When he bent his head to kiss her, she met him halfway. No, more than that, for she pulled her hands free of his and wound them around his neck. For this moment she would forget her uncle and her mother. For this moment there was nothing but Harry and herself. For this moment she had no doubts at all about what she wished to do.

If Harry was surprised, he did not show it. His arms slid around her back to hold her and to let his hand twine itself within her hair. The kiss, begun as something gentle and reassuring, became much more. A demand. A promise. A pledge.

And when he undid the pins in her hair she reached to undo his cravat. He paused to smile down at her, a twinkle in his eyes as he said, "Eager, are you?"

She nodded, not trusting herself to speak. But he must have read something there that pleased him for he smiled tenderly and touched her lips with his fingertip. Then he kissed her again.

"Do you not wish me to be?" she asked softly.

In answer, he lifted her onto the bed and for the next hour they had no thoughts for anyone but each other. He was a gentle and inventive lover.

Later, as they lay tangled together on the bed, Prudence felt such a closeness and longing for Harry that it frightened her. She traced a pattern on his chest with her fingertip. She drew in her breath and forced herself to speak.

"I need to tell you that it's all right that you have to go back to France," she said. "I understand."

He pulled back and tilted up her chin so that she was forced to look at him. "What the devil do you mean by that?" he demanded in patent bewilderment. "Are you so eager to be rid of me, then? Particularly after what we have just shared?"

"No! Of course not!"

"Then why?"

She hesitated. "Because I have thought about you and what matters to you and I understand a little better now, I think, how much you need to do this. I cannot, I shall never like it, but I understand."

To her shock, he chuckled. And when she stiffened he soothed her with a gentle touch on her back. He kissed her forehead and said, "I, on the other hand, have come to the conclusion that I ought not to go."

That startled her. As much as her statement had startled him. "Why not?"

He smiled at her. "My brother George pointed out that perhaps it was, at least in part, vanity to believe that I was the only one who could do what needed to be done. It has taken me several days to realize that perhaps he is right. That perhaps I would even be putting the mission in jeopardy by insisting on going myself."

"Lord Darton told you not to go?"

Prudence could not hide her surprise. Harry grinned. "My brother has undergone some changes of late. I think that I like them, but they are rather unexpected, I will allow."

Prudence snuggled closer to her husband. Into his chest she said, "Well, whatever the reason, I can only be grateful that he keeps you with me a little longer."

Harry raised his eyebrows at that. "A little? Why?

Do you intend to leave me? For I tell you that not only do I not mean to return to France but I have been thinking that I could be of more use here at home. Indeed, I have been thinking that between us we can do a great deal of good. We shall set ourselves up in a neat little establishment and give parties. Between us we shall charm everyone—diplomats and soldiers alike."

She looked at him doubtfully. "But have we the funds to afford our own establishment?"

He burst out laughing and kissed her for several delightful moments again. "My poor Prudence, did you think me bereft of funds? Is that why you went to work for Lord Brandon? Because you feared you must support us?"

Prudence did not dare answer the last part of his question so she focused instead on the first. "I did think you might be short of funds. Until you sold out, at any rate, and collected your prize money," she answered honestly.

Harry smiled indulgently. "I have a bit more than that. An aunt who was beforehand with the world left me a tidy sum that will allow us not luxury but comfort. That combined with what I shall receive if I continue to work at the Horse Guards ought to suffice. Never fear, I shan't make you sing for your supper like a gypsy."

Prudence blushed at this reminder of their adventures. She could not, she positively could not meet his eyes! And then he surprised her again.

"There was one other thing," he said diffidently.

"If it is about Lord Brandon, I cannot stop going to help him."

She said it with defiance in her voice as well as a tremor of fear. To her surprise he was not angry. He sighed but said, "No, I rather thought you would not. I cannot like it, but neither shall I try to forbid it. In the end I have come to understand that this is somehow important to you. I must trust that someday you will trust me sufficiently to confide to me why."

And that, of course, made Prudence feel more guilty than ever. But she had promised Sir Thomas and he had impressed upon her the importance of what they were doing.

"Someday," she whispered.

"Good. But it is another matter entirely that I wish to speak to you about," he said, and there was that odd note to Harry's voice again.

Prudence looked at him and spied mischief in his eyes. "Oh?" she asked warily.

"Well, I was thinking that perhaps we should have some children. Any children we have, you see, would learn the best of both our skills."

Prudence wanted to laugh at his nonsense, but the words, the notion took her breath away. "Children?" she echoed.

Harry frowned, worried by her response. "Don't you wish for children?" he asked, the diffidence real this time.

Her brow cleared and she hugged him all the tighter as she said, fervently, "Yes, Harry, oh yes!"

There was very little conversation between them after that though neither, it was to be noted, got much sleep that night.

In a small but respectable hotel in another part of town something entirely different was happening. Frederick Baines was engaged in reading one of his favorite books when he had an unexpected visitor. His valet permitted the heavily veiled woman to enter with some trepidation. But the moment they were alone and the woman removed her veil Baines greeted her with both recognition and warm delight.

"My dear Lady Marland, how do you do? We had heard about your protector's death and I wondered when you would make your way to England. Or if you would. Come. Sit by the fire. Tell me everything about your journey."

Lady Marland smiled at him and took the seat he indicated. She smoothed her skirts and took her time about answering him. When she did, it was not in the least what he expected.

"It is about my daughter's husband, Colonel Harry Langford. He intends to go back to France and I wish you to stop him."

Frederick Baines froze. He stared at her. Finally he managed to echo her words. "Stop him?"

Lady Marland explained. Baines slowly sank into the seat opposite her. When she was done telling him about her daughter's husband, Baines said carefully, "But you do not even know why he is supposed to go back to France. How can you know whether you ought to stop him? And why come to me?"

She looked at him then, her eyes wide with innocence. "Why Freddy, I know you can find out anything you choose to find out, do anything you choose to do. My daughter is dreadfully unhappy over this and I thought you would be pleased to help me."

He started laughing. He could not help himself. She stared at him a trifle bewildered, a trifle angry. In the frostiest of voices she said, "I am pleased to have been able to amuse you so thoroughly but, sir, I wish you will tell me why you are so amused."

Baines sobered, though not entirely. Still, he tried.

"I, er, have some knowledge of the circumstances you are speaking about," he said. "The difficulty is that someone needs to go to France and deal with a certain problem there. If Colonel Langford is not to go, who should? Unless you are volunteering?"

Grace Marland stared at him. Instinctively she shook her head. He merely stared back at her. She rose to her feet and moved a few steps away then turned to look at Frederick Baines. Her face was pale and her voice held uncertainty as she said, "You do not know what you ask of me. I had not thought to go back there. Ever again. I had been looking forward to returning to my home in Philadelphia."

Baines regarded her gravely. "Then go home. We shall contrive. Harry shall contrive. He is a clever and courageous young man. I have great hopes that he will succeed in his mission and return unscathed."

But Lady Marland shook her head. "No. I cannot do that to my daughter. I have failed her as a mother all these years, I cannot fail her now. Very well, I shall go back to France in his place. What is it I shall need to do?"

She half-expected him to grin with triumph. But this was Frederick Baines and all he did was rise to his feet, take her hand, and say, gravely, "I am in awe, as always, of your courage."

Lady Marland yanked free her hand, and said, crossly, "Fustian! Just tell me when and where and how I go and what lines I am to learn this time."

But he shook his head. "Oh, no, my dear. I do believe I shall go with you. We can learn our lines together, on the way."

Chapter 25

Prudence dared let no more time go by. She called upon Sir Thomas early the next morning. He took one look at her face and drew her into his study. This morning he wasted no time on pleasantries. Nor did she.

"Lord Brandon has made his proposal, sir. He wishes me to arrange an expedition involving every member of the Langford family, including the children. I am to ride separately with Harry."

"When?"

"He suggested next week. I am to tell him the precise day and time and he will, he said, arrange everything else."

"Excellent! You've done very well. And the letter? How did he respond to the letter?"

"With glee, I should say. And the moment after he had it, that was when he began to ask if I was happy. Which led to his proposal to make Harry the heir to Lord Darton's title. I thought it best you know as soon as possible. You told me to agree to whatever he proposed, but surely this is too dangerous?"

Sir Thomas hesitated. "Perhaps, perhaps not. I believe it is possible to protect the Langfords. In any event, I should need their consent before we proceeded. But for the moment, go and tell Lord Brandon that arrangements are in hand. We can always tell him the plans had to be changed if the Langfords will not agree or I cannot guarantee their safety."

Prudence hesitated. He leaned forward and patted

her hand. "Trust me, my dear. I will make certain that nothing happens to any of you."

Oddly enough, Prudence found that she did trust the man. She could not have said why, but years of moving in diplomatic circles had taught her how to tell when someone was telling the truth and how to judge a man's character. Sir Thomas Levenger was, she realized, a man she would trust with her life. And with Harry's.

She would have left then but as Sir Thomas escorted her to the front door, two more guests arrived. One was a gentleman she had never met but it was evident he and Sir Thomas knew each other well. He had, moreover, a companion she did recognize.

"Mother?" Prudence said, staring in disbelief. "What are you doing here?"

Lady Marland seemed equally taken aback.

"Perhaps we should, er, retire to my study again," Sir Thomas said hastily.

All too aware of the servants, they agreed with alacrity. There, in the study, with the door firmly closed, Sir Thomas waved them to seats. He looked at the gentleman. "Freddy?"

The man lifted one shoulder and shrugged. "Lady Marland has a suggestion. One, I might add, that has my support."

"Oh?"

That one word was sufficient to tell Prudence that Sir Thomas reposed just as much trust in this gentleman as she reposed in him.

"Lady Marland has suggested that she go back to France in place of Colonel Langford. I have offered to go with her."

Instantly Prudence was on her feet. "Mother? You cannot mean to do this!"

Lady Marland looked up at her daughter, her tranquillity undisturbed. "Why not? It is a part of France where I have never been so it is most unlikely that I should be recognized. But I have sufficient connections that I could pass easily where I will. Nor am I encumbered by an injury, as your husband is. Why should I not go in his place?"

Sir Thomas grinned at her. "Lady Marland, you have all my admiration and respect," he said.

"Fustian!" she exclaimed, but it was patent that she was pleased.

"It does make sense," the other gentleman said. "I know the system as well as anyone and with Lady Marland to ease our way, we should be able to go and return swiftly."

Sir Thomas nodded. "How soon can you leave?" he asked.

"The day after tomorrow," Lady Marland replied. "Hugo has already made certain arrangements on our behalf." At Prudence's cry of protest, she looked at her and said, with a wry smile, "The sooner Mr. Baines and I go, the sooner we shall return. And now, Sir Thomas, we must take our leave of you. There is much to be done."

He nodded. To Prudence he added, "Wait here, my dear. I shall show your mother and Freddy out and that will give you time to compose yourself. In any event, it would be best if you were not all seen leaving together."

Lord Brandon seemed most pleased to have Prudence arrive early. Her head was still awhirl with seeing her mother. All thoughts of the other matter she had planned with Sir Thomas went straight out of her mind. But Lord Brandon had not forgotten. He eyed her oddly a number of times and then finally raised the question himself

"Have you given any thought," he asked Prudence, "to what we discussed the other day?"

That recalled her to the whole issue of the Langfords and Lord Brandon's plans for them. She hesitated. That was natural, wasn't it? She could feel her color rising and that, too, she hoped would lend verisimilitude to the part she was playing.

At last she said, with a hint of diffidence in her voice, "I did suggest an outing. They are thinking the matter over and it is no easy task to arrange for everyone to be able to go on the same day. But at least they did not dismiss the notion out of hand."

"But?"

Prudence raised her eyes to meet his and let them fill with doubt. "But I am not entirely certain I should be doing this. They have tried to be kind to me."

Lord Brandon came and took her hands, as he had done the last time they spoke. "My dear child! Your sentiments are creditable but perhaps a trifle naive? You say they have tried to be kind to you. If that were true, would they not have succeeded? Oh, I know all too well how that family is! How they look at one with that pitying smile, how they pretend to concern even as they rip one's character to shreds when speaking to each other. How they are incapable of forgiving mistakes in others but expect complete forgiveness themselves. Oh, yes, I know the Langford family well. And I do not think they are kind to you, I do not think so at all."

She looked at him. She had no need to counterfeit confusion as she asked him, "How? How do you know so much about them when I, who live in Lord Darton's house, cannot see so clearly?"

He gave a short laugh and half turned away. There was bitterness in Lord Brandon's voice as he said, "There was a time when I was much involved with the family. Indeed, I had once thought to wed the late Lord Darton's sister. But he laughed at me. Forbade me the house, for he was her guardian then. Know that family? Oh, yes, I know that family. I have made it my business to do so. To watch them, to try to understand. Trust me, my dear, I shall have no hesitation in helping you rid yourself of the burden of their existence. Trust me and you shall have the position, the money you so dearly wish for. And I shall be rid of a family that has plagued me for far too many years."

Prudence touched his sleeve hesitantly. "But you will not harm Harry, will you, sir? He has not hurt you, surely?"

Lord Brandon could not at once answer. But after a moment he regained his composure and put his hand over hers. He even managed to smile, albeit the smile seemed a little perfunctory to her.

"You need not worry, my dear. I have taken your feelings into account and should not dream of leaving you to manage on your own."

A shiver went up Prudence's spine at these words. They seemed to have an ominous ring to them. But she pretended to believe the reassurance Lord Brandon appeared to give her. She, too, smiled and if her smile was no more real than his, well, they both pretended otherwise. And soon they were back at work on his memoirs.

The entire family gathered at Philip Langford's town house two days later. Even Lord Darton was given an unaccustomed invitation to join the group, as were all of the wives. Indeed, they seemed to fill the drawing room as the Langfords looked at one another and at Sir Thomas Levenger and his wife with great curiosity.

"There is," Sir Thomas said, "a matter with which I need your help. It has to do with the man who I believe arranged the death of your parents, Lord and Lady Darton."

Quite naturally, there was an uproar. Sir Thomas simply waited until the noise diminished, refusing to answer the questions demanded of him until he was ready.

"I will not tell you his name yet," Sir Thomas said with creditable calm. "But I believe we have a way to catch him in the act of attempting to kill again. To kill all of you. If you are willing to help I believe we can deal with him once and for all."

This time the uproar abated faster, for the Langfords were an intelligent group. "And just what do we need to do?" Philip asked dryly.

Sir Thomas explained. He explained in great detail what he wished them to do and how he intended to protect them. He talked about anarchists and the men he had hired to follow and observe the contact that went between them and the man behind the killing. But he carefully named no names.

There were objections, of course. But in the end, all agreed. For the sake of catching the person who murdered Lord and Lady Darton, they would do as Sir Thomas asked.

"Thank you," he said gravely. "You do more than help to catch the man who arranged the deaths of your parents. You are helping, I believe, to catch a traitor. If we cannot prove treason we may, at least, prove another crime that will put paid to all his endeavors, including those that betray our country to the French."

There was a great deal of speculation as they left and Prudence was hard put not to speak. But she did not dare. For if she did, she might let slip something that Sir Thomas felt essential to keep quiet.

It was Harry, of course, who noticed her reticence and commented upon it. "Have you no theories?" he asked her in the carriage on the way home.

"How the devil should she have any theories?" Lord Darton demanded irritably. "How should any of us? I cannot like this notion. If it were anyone but Sir Thomas asking this of us I should have refused. As it is, I shall not rest easy until the matter is over and done with."

"None of us shall," Lady Darton agreed with a shudder.

That was a sentiment to which Prudence could whole-heartedly agree and she did so. But still Harry stared at her as though he could sense there was more to be said. So what could she do, when they reached Lord Darton's town house, but distract him with some of what she had seen in the book that Emily and Juliet had shown her?

Chapter 26

Precisely as Lord Brandon had advised, all the carriages met at Lord Darton's town house in the morning. Every member of the Langford family was there. It was too cold a day for a picnic but another entertainment had been arranged. Or so Prudence had told his lordship several days before.

Brandon himself was nowhere to be seen. He had closed up his town house and given out that he meant to retire to his country seat for a time. Neither Prudence nor Sir Thomas believed him. Still, they pretended to be oblivious to any threat—either from him or anyone else.

It was all a sham, of course. The adults had been told as little as possible, but enough so that they knew something of what was happening. Naturally they were nervous and that emotion conveyed itself to the children, who became even more restless than usual as a result.

Every one of the parents would have left their children home, had it been possible. But the pretense of normality was essential. If Lord and Lady Darton brought their children, so must the rest. It was a measure of the trust the Langfords placed in Sir Thomas that they agreed to do this for him when he asked.

As he stood in the drawing room filled with adults and children, Sir Thomas said, slowly and carefully so that he could not be misunderstood, "I thank you. This is a matter that touches on the security of England. I know there is a risk but we have taken steps, every possible measure, to insure that it is as small as possible. And by doing this, by having you draw our quarry out into the open, we hope to trap a cunning traitor we have not been able to catch any other way."

So at something like half an hour past the appointed time, the Langfords all emerged from Lord Darton's front doorway. As arranged between them, the adults formed a shield around the children. It was done so skillfully that an onlooker would have sworn all was confusion and that it had happened by chance. But it did not. The children were carefully surrounded by adults. And when they reached the carriages, the children were still shielded, the men alert for strangers and any possible danger.

From an upstairs window, Sir Thomas Levenger and his wife, Agatha, watched. She clutched at his arm. "I pray that nothing goes wrong," she said anxiously.

He put his hand over hers. "Every possible precaution has been taken. We must hope they will prove sufficient."

As arranged, Harry and Prudence moved to the lead carriage. They were, after all, supposed to ride alone. Only Prudence knew why and she quailed at the notion of exposing Lord Brandon's plans and her apparent complicity to Harry's family.

Prudence held her breath as Harry handed her up into the carriage. It was a cold day for a ride in such an open vehicle. But somehow she did not think they would be going very far and, in any event, considering what was about to happen, such considerations seemed unimportant.

Suddenly the peaceful morning was shattered by cries of "death to tyranny!"

Men rushed out of hiding places to toss objects at the carriages. Even as Prudence turned to look, to see if the others were safe, a crack rang out and Harry pulled on her arm, pulling her down and out of the carriage just as something tore into the fabric of the coach behind her head.

Harry meant to catch her, she had no doubt of that. But something happened and he fell slightly off balance. Prudence tumbled to the ground and her head struck something hard as she fell.

All around her was chaos. Men were running, shouting, more gunshots rang out and a bullet struck perilously close to where she lay. She tried to rise only to be thrust down again with a harsh command from a familiar voice.

"Stay down!"

Prudence did not argue with Wilkins nor ask how he came to be there. Instead, from her position close to the ground, she watched as he ran toward several men who were struggling together. On the top step, by the front door of Lord Darton's town house, she could see Sir Thomas Levenger looking for someone. Suddenly he moved forward, taking the steps two and three at a time.

Prudence turned to look where he was heading and she saw Harry dragging someone forward. He seemed completely undeterred by the way his injured leg still hampered him. She drew in a deep breath as she realized the man he held was Lord Brandon. He was struggling against Harry's grasp and she could not help but feel glad to see two of Harry's brothers rush forward to help him subdue the man.

Now Wilkins was back at her side and helped Prudence to her feet. "I'm very sorry. Didn't mean no offense, but it were safer you stayed on t'ground."

She looked at him and smiled. "Believe me, Wilkins, I am very grateful that you did push me back down."

Prudence joined the Langford women, all standing huddled together, their children still shielded within the circle they formed. She looked to Sir Thomas to see what was happening, whether he seemed pleased or not. He was with Harry and the other Langford men helping to bind Lord Brandon's arms. A group of men she could only suppose to be Bow Street Runners had another group surrounded.

She could not repress a shudder of relief when she saw the last of the villains bundled into hackneys and setting off down the street, the sturdy Runners with them. Only then, when the carriages were all out of sight, did the Langfords go inside. The children were sent up to the nursery to chatter excitedly about the morning's adventure. The grown-ups repaired to the drawing room and a glass of wine each to steady their frayed nerves.

"I do hope," Lord Darton said severely, "that you mean to tell us what just happened, Sir Thomas."

The elder barrister smiled. "I certainly shall," he replied. "I am aware that I have sorely tried your patience. But it is no exaggeration when I say that it was of the greatest importance. Both to our country and to your own family."

Quietly he began to explain. "You didn't know it, no one did and that was to their advantage, but your parents, Lord and Lady Darton, had the courage to try to help us trap traitors. They had obtained a letter written, we believed to Lord Brandon, by Napoleon Bonaparte. He did everything in his power to discredit them. But far worse, I believe he arranged the carriage accident that killed them. I have no proof," he added, holding up a hand to forestall questions, "but it is what I have believed for these ten years."

"Ten years!" George exclaimed. "And you did nothing about it?"

A look of pain crossed the barrister's face. "I tried," he said in a voice scarcely above a whisper. "But until Prudence became my ally in this venture, all my efforts failed. It was she who managed to get into Lord Brandon's confidence sufficiently to cause him to betray himself to her."

"Prudence?" Several voices murmured her name in surprise.

"Then why did he shoot at her?" Harry protested. "For I'll swear she was his target."

Sir Thomas nodded. He clasped his hands behind his back. "She was the only one who could have told what he had said to her. The only one, he thought, who knew that he was behind today's attempt to murder all of you. Were she dead, the bombs thrown would, he hoped, be attributed to anarchists, of whom there are too many in London these days. That was why he had to make certain she did not survive."

There were a number of visible shudders. "You mean those were bombs they were hurling at us?" George demanded indignantly.

"Patently not, if they did not destroy us," James replied with a poor attempt at humor.

"But they were meant to be?" Philip hazarded.

Sir Thomas nodded. "I have had a man watching Lord Brandon's household and he followed the messenger used to carry word to the anarchists and back again. We managed to get a man inside their group and he replaced the real bombs with substitutes that could do no harm. The only real danger this morning was from Lord Brandon. I thought he would wish to make certain of the death of the only person who could connect him to the anarchists. The messenger," he added quietly, "is already dead."

"How could you know he would be here at all?" Harry asked. "It seems an unlikely risk for him to have taken. He could easily have had someone else attempt to murder Prudence, if the bombs failed to do so."

Sir Thomas shrugged. "I could not be certain, but I thought he would come himself. It seemed unlike Lord Brandon to trust the task to anyone else."

There was silence as they all pondered what had just been said. Prudence and Sir Thomas exchanged rueful looks. When, they both wondered, would it occur to the others to speak about her role in all of this?

Not very long. Abruptly Athenia turned to Prudence and demanded, "Is that why you went to work in Lord Brandon's household? At Sir Thomas's behest?"

How she wished she could say yes! But Prudence was not a coward and so she straightened her shoulders unconsciously and replied, "No, I went to work for him because of another matter."

What had begun as hopeful smiles now turned to disapproving scowls. Sir Thomas shook his head reprovingly, though whether at the Langfords or at Prudence none of them could have said.

"She went there for another purpose but it still touched on Langford honor," he told them. "Explain, my dear, about France and overhearing about the letter."

Harry turned a piercing gaze on Prudence and she carefully avoided meeting his eyes. How to explain why she could not tell him what she was doing? Instead she put her attention into trying to simply explain to the entire family the reasoning that led her to take the steps she did.

"In France there was mention of a letter. I thought that it seemed as if Harry believed Bonaparte had sent it to your father, the late Lord Darton. But the Frenchman made it evident that the letter had been meant for someone else. I thought it a curious interchange and bent my mind to the task of determining whether I could guess who the person might be. There was," she added half-apologetically, "a great deal of time to think, you see."

She paused and took a deep breath before she went on. "When I thought of the people who had moved in the same circles as my uncle, I found my mind returning again and again to Lord Brandon and some of the odd things I had heard him say, over the years. I found I could not dismiss the notion that it might have been he to whom the letter was originally sent. I thought that if I went to work for him, helping him with his memoirs, that I might find proof that he was. Then Sir Thomas spoke with me and asked that I take a somewhat different direction in my dealings with Lord Brandon. Today is the result of that."

There was a stunned silence and then a noisy burst of approving words, with Lord Darton insisting upon toasting Prudence. Only Harry was not pleased. Under cover of the general noise and with the appearance of a loving gesture, he put an arm around her waist and pulled her to him. He held on tight and would not let her go as he demanded, in a voice that carried to her ears only, "How dare you take such a risk? How dare you not tell me you were doing so?"

"Because you might have tried to stop me," she answered in return. "Because my suspicions were only that and I would not condemn any man to the censure of his fellows without some kind of proof. Because it was something I had to do."

"And you could not do it with me, could not tell me because I, your husband, am a cripple!"

And with those harsh words he released her waist and rose to his feet. That he meant to leave her, to leave all of them, she could not doubt. Prudence rose to her feet as well. Her voice was loud and clear and cut through all the other noise to bring silence to the room.

"Cripple? Only if you believe so, Harry. I see a man capable of doing almost anything he wishes. The only thing you cannot be is a soldier and I am not certain that is the best use of your talents anyway."

Now it was an appalled silence that held the room in sway as everyone waited for Harry's angry answer. It was not long in coming.

"A soldier is all I have ever wanted to be!"

It was as though he flung the words at her, like a gauntlet, daring her to fling them back at him. She would not have disappointed him save that someone else spoke first.

It was, to everyone's surprise, Sir Thomas. There

was an edge of reproval to his voice as he said, "And do you think that is the only value you have? Foolish puppy! I have heard time and again this past month that you are of more value in the Horse Guards than ever you were in the field! Do you know what it means to Wellington to have a man here who knows what it is like for him? Who understands the importance of supplies? Who will recognize what might occur next?"

Harry gaped at Sir Thomas and then Athenia addressed him. Her voice was more gentle than any, save George, could ever remembering hearing her speak.

"There can be no doubt as to your courage, Harry. Nor that you would be in the field if you could."

Both Philip and James came to stand beside him.

"You are a fool if you think we value you less because of your injury," Philip said, clouting his brother on the shoulder.

James chuckled. "Yes, but then we always knew he was." When Harry glared at him he added, "Look at your bride, Harry. We have. And we can tell you she does not look at you as if she thought you a matter for pity. Indeed, I should say there was a far warmer emotion there."

Harry colored up, but he did look at Prudence and at once she came toward him, a mixture of softness and exasperation in both her eyes and her voice.

"Do you think me such a fool, Harry, that I would only see your leg and not the man you are? That I fell in love with you because of how fast you could run?"

"Love?" Harry echoed uncertainly. "You are saying that you love me?"

"Well, of course she does!" Emily and Juliet and Lady Levenger all exclaimed at precisely the same moment.

Now they both colored up. Prudence took another step closer to Harry and his brothers stepped away, for which she was grateful. There were things, she realized, that she needed to say. And it was not going to be easy to find the words to say them. She took a deep breath and tried.

"I owe you an apology," she began. "You are right. I should have told you at the start what I suspected. And what I meant to do. I should have given you the chance to help me. I am beginning to realize that is part of loving someone. But I have never known, you see, what it was to be able to lean on someone for support. Never had anyone care enough to wish me to do so."

"I care enough. I want you to," Harry said, in a voice that shook.

Prudence looked at him. Now her own voice shook as she asked, "Truly?"

When he nodded and held his arms open to her, she went straight into them. Behind her, Lord Darton cleared his throat in warning. Once again, however, Sir Thomas forestalled everyone.

"Perhaps the two of you had best continue this conversation in private," the barrister suggested with some amusement.

Accompanied by the teasing comments of his entire family, Prudence let Harry lead her out of the drawing room and down the hallway to his room. She went quite willingly. There were, after all, more words to be said, more assurances to be given. And received. Afterward? Well, there were still a great many drawings in that book and sooner or later she meant to try every one.

Epilogue

The crowd in the drawing room was a large one even though it was almost morning and most of the guests invited to tonight's masquerade ball were already gone. This group was comprised almost entirely of members of the Langford family. In the center stood a radiant lady and her husband beside her. He wore a colonel's uniform, she wore the robes of a Moroccan prince. Early on in the evening someone had dubbed him the sentimental soldier and it had stuck. Now Harry raised his glass of champagne and everyone else did likewise.

"To our new home, may it be as loving a one as each of you have made of your own."

"Here, here!"

"What word of your mother?" Emily asked Prudence for, in the end, the journey had not been kept quiet from the brothers and their wives.

Harry answered for her. With an arm fixed firmly around her waist, he said, "Prudence's mother, along with Frederick Baines, is on her way back to England. They ought to arrive in a few days."

"Yes, but where are George and Athenia?" James demanded, almost petulantly. "I should have expected them to be here! They consider it their duty to oversee every family event, after all."

Emily and Philip looked at one another and it was he who said, carefully not meeting anyone's eyes, "I collect they, er, have gone away to, er, spend some time alone together."

"Alone together? Why the devil should they want to do that?" James persisted.

It was Emily who said, with a significant glance to Lady Levenger and Juliet and Prudence, "I collect it was Athenia who arranged everything. After she borrowed the book."

"Book?" Philip said, giving his wife a surprised look. "What book did you lend them, my dear?"

But she refused to answer. Juliet and Prudence were hard pressed not to laugh out loud. To Philip, Emily said, "It's not important, dear."

It was Sir Thomas who diverted everyone's attention, however. "And how are things at the Horse Guards, Harry?" He asked, with a careless air that fooled no one.

Harry grinned at the barrister. "You were quite right, sir. I am needed far more than ever I was in the Peninsula. I have hopes of doing Wellington more good here than I did him there. And since we helped to capture Lord Brandon and he killed himself, one avenue of information leaking to France has ended and I am even more welcome at the Horse Guards than I was before."

Sir Thomas nodded approvingly. "As you should be, my boy, as you should be." He paused and turned his attention to Prudence. "And you, my dear? I hear you are cutting quite a swath through the *ton*. Your wit is everywhere admired and the ladies have nothing bad to say about you. Even your attire tonight was accounted something of a coup rather than the scandal I'll wager your husband told you it would be. All in all, a remarkable accomplishment, I assure you! At this rate we shall hear of you being appointed ambassador to some major post at no great time in the future."

Prudence laughed. "Perhaps. Save for the simple fact that a woman shall never be declared an official ambassador," she replied easily. "It is fortunate that

I am quite content to stay at Harry's side and preside over his social affairs instead of my own."

There was general laughter over that comment and good-natured roasting. It was Harry who said, "The day you are content to preside over my affairs instead of your own I shall know you have gone into a serious decline, my love!"

There was such warmth in his eyes that Prudence could not but feel relieved when the other Langfords departed. She dearly loved her husband's family but she wanted to be alone with Harry. She had, after all, a surprise for him.

Although all her things had been lost when she was pushed overboard on the ship, she and Mrs. Wise, between them, had managed to duplicate another ensemble she had brought back from Morocco with her. Only this one was nothing like the men's robes she had swathed around herself to pass as a man, nothing like the ones she wore now. No, this ensemble was one worn only by women in Morocco and even then only in the most private of circumstances.

A smile lit Prudence's face as she contemplated Harry's expression when first he saw her in this other attire. He regarded her quizzically. All she would say aloud, however, was, "Give me perhaps fifteen minutes and then come upstairs. I've something I wish to show you."

He hesitated and she added softly, "Alain."

Immediately his eyes glowed and he grinned. "As you wish, my love," he said with a bow.

And then, before he could ask any questions, for they would surely put her to the blush, Prudence hurried out of the room. The Moroccan ensemble waited and so did her heart, for all these months of marriage had still not accustomed her to the joy of being with Harry nor the pleasures to be found in the marriage bed. But Prudence meant to sample them for all the rest of her life.

Author's Note

Look for the return of the inimitable Miss Tibbles in *Miss Tibbles Investigates*. What happens when she is invited to spend a quiet week at the country home of one of her former charges? Of course, nothing is ever quiet around Miss Tibbles.

Look for news of upcoming books at my website: http://www.sff.net/people/april.kihlstrom.

I love hearing from readers. I can be reached by E-mail at: april.kihlstrom@sff.net

Or write to me at: April Kihlstrom
                      Suite 240
                      532 Old Marlton Pike
                      Cherry Hill, NJ 08053

Please send a SASE for a newsletter and reply.